Patrick

Andy Griffiths discovered a talent for annoying his parents at an early age. Since then he has gone on to annoy many other people including friends, neighbours, teachers and complete strangers with his silly noises, idiotic questions, stupid comments, bad jokes, inappropriate behaviour and pointless stories. His most recent book, *Just Tricking!*, was published in 1997.

Terry Denton hates writing illustrator biographies. He finds them annoying. So he draws them. The problem with this is . . . what do you draw about yourself? Well, what about your most annoying points? Terry has four of them.

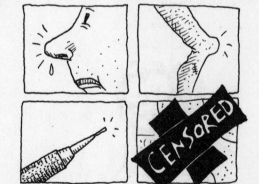

Oh, by the way, Andy is right. He is very annoying. Typical author!

Also by Andy Griffiths
and illustrated by Terry Denton

Just Tricking!
Just Annoying!
Just Stupid !
Just Crazy!
Just Disgusting!

And by Andy Griffiths

The Day My Bum Went Psycho
Zombie Bums From Uranus

VISIT ANDY AT HIS
WEBSITE!
www.andygriffiths.com.au

JUST ANNOYING!

ANDY GRIFFITHS

WITH ILLUSTRATIONS BY
TERRY DENTON.

PAN
Pan Macmillan Australia

First published 1998 in Pan by Pan Macmillan Australia Pty Limited
St Martins Tower, 31 Market St, Sydney

Reprinted 1998 (twice), 1999 (three times), 2000 (four times), 2001 (five times),
2002 (three times), 2003 (twice), 2004

National Library of Australia
cataloguing-in-publication data:

Griffiths, Andrew, 1961– .
Just annoying.

ISBN 0 330 36078 7.

1. Short stories, Australian. I. Denton, Terry, 1950– . II. Title.

A823.3

Typeset in 12/16pt New Aster by Post Pre-press Group
Printed in Australia by McPherson's Printing Group

Contents

ARE WE THERE YET?

ad?'

'Yes?'

'Are we there yet?'

'No.'

'Now?'

'No.'

'Now?'

'For goodness sakes!' growls Dad. 'Will you stop it!'

'Alright,' I say. 'Don't get your knickers in a knot.'

KNOTTED KNICKERS.

We've been in the car for two days now. Mum and Dad are at breaking point.

Don't get me wrong. I don't *want* them to get mad at me—it just happens.

Like it or not, when you go on a long drive

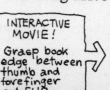

INTERACTIVE MOVIE!

Grasp book edge between thumb and forefinger and FLIP.

FAVOURITE
FLY
RESTING
SPOTS.

there are times when you just have to stop.

And my parents do not like it.

But what's the alternative?

Do they want me to starve to death? To wet my pants? To be sick all over the back seat?

I think any of these would be a lot more annoying and inconvenient than the few stops it takes to prevent them. I'm actually doing them a favour.

Mum and Dad should save their energy for really annoying things. Like the fly that has been buzzing around in the car for the last half hour. It's driving me mental. I'm going to do us all a big favour. I'm going to get rid of it.

I wind the window down. The fly jumps away.

It's hiding, just waiting for me to wind the window back up again.

I have to lure it out.

I start doing my best fly-call.

'Bzzzz! Bzzzzzzz! Bzzzzzzzzzzzzz!'

Still no fly. Have to do it louder.

'BZZZZZZ! BZZZZZZZZ! BZZZZZZZZZ!'

'Andy!' yells Dad. 'I can't concentrate with you making that stupid noise. Do you want

BABY
WILL JUST
LOVE YOUR
OLD DEAD
FLIES

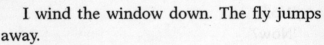
BZzzzzz

us to have an accident? Do you want us all to be killed?'

I hate it when Dad asks dumb questions like that. What does he expect me to say? 'Yes, Dad, I want us to have an accident. I want us all to be killed.'

But I don't say that. It might cause Dad to have an accident. We might all be killed.

'Alright, Dad,' I say instead. 'Don't get your knickers in a knot.'

'And stop telling me not to get my knickers in a knot!' he explodes.

'Okay,' I say. 'Don't get your trousers in a twist.'

Dad hunches over the steering wheel. His knuckles whiten. Tiny drops of perspiration appear on the back of his neck.

He knows he's been outsmarted once again. It must be frustrating for him having a son as clever as me. It must be hard knowing that he can never win.

The fly lazily cruises in front of my eyes. It's asking for trouble. Well, it's come to the right man.

I once saw a movie where the door of an aeroplane opened mid-air and everybody was sucked out by the vacuum it created. I

Tying your knickers in knots.
Lesson: 12
The double overhand knot.
1. Take a large pair of knickers.
2.
3.
Pot them on.

FAVOURITE FLY RESTING SPOTS

ZZZzz 3

To accompany the MOVIE try making your own sound effects.

don't need a vacuum quite that powerful, but maybe if I open and close the door I'll be able to create one strong enough to suck the fly out.

I squeeze the door handle as carefully and slowly as I can so that it doesn't make any noise. I swing it open, then shut.

Open, shut.

Open, shut.

'What do you think you're doing?' screams Dad.

'I'm creating a vacuum,' I say.

'What?'

'A vacuum! I'm trying to get a fly out of the car.'

FOR THE WORLD'S BEST ANNOYING TRICK TURN TO PAGE 38.

'Shut the door! And keep it shut!' shouts Dad. 'I'm warning you. If you don't behave yourself, I'll stop the car and you can get out and walk. Do you understand?'

'But, Dad . . .' I say.

'No buts! Do you understand?'

'Yes, Dad.'

Dad's knuckles are really white now. He's gripping the steering wheel so hard that his bones are practically breaking through his skin.

I hear a buzz. It's coming from behind me.

4

The vacuum didn't work. I turn around but I can't see the fly. Hang on—the noise is coming from outside.

I undo my seatbelt and kneel up on the seat to get a better view.

There's this crazy-looking guy riding an old black Harley. He's got a long red beard, a black bowl-shaped helmet and a pair of old-fashioned plastic riding goggles. They make him look like a fly. And his motorbike sounds like one. Only much louder.

Suddenly the fly shoots across the window.
Showdown time!

I try to cup it in my left hand and hook it out of the window.

That's my plan, anyway.

But the fly has other ideas. It skates across the window to the far corner. And then back again. I'm chasing the fly back and forth across the window when I notice that the bikie is making hand signals.

He thinks I'm waving to him!
I wave.
He waves back.
I wave again.
He waves back again.
We're best friends now.

I'm looking for the page of jokes about Mechanical Birds.

FOR ALL MECHANICAL BIRD JOKES, SEE PAGE 79.

Are we nearly there yet?

QUIET, Mum.

A fly? This is a story about a fly. WOW!

5

'Stop waving,' says Dad. 'Sit down and put your seatbelt back on.'

'But he waved first,' I say.

'Don't annoy bikies,' says Dad. 'I don't want any trouble.'

'I'm not annoying him—I was just being friendly.'

'Sit down!'

'Okay, okay, don't get your knickers in a knot.'

I told you already. Don't put your head out the window.

I give one last wave to Bike-man, but he's pulling into a service station and doesn't see me.

I feel like I've lost my best friend.

I notice a movement out of the corner of my eye.

I look up. The fly is on the roof. It's taunting me. It buzzes again.

'Andy,' says Dad, 'you're pushing your luck!'

'It wasn't me,' I say. 'It was the fly!'

I have to get rid of this fly. And quickly. Before it gets rid of me.

I reach up and try to cup it with my hand.

It jumps to the left.

I try again.

It jumps to the right and then heads

HARMONIOUS HAPPY HOLIDAY TIP #4.

When you fill up with

Petrol, don't insert the nozzle in your brother's ear.

I'd love to play the fly in the movie of this book.

6

BZZZ OFF

towards the front windscreen, daring me to come after it.

I unbuckle my seatbelt and dive into the front seat. I catch the fly in mid-air.

'HOWZAT?' I yell.

I'm lying with my head in Mum's lap and my legs all over the steering wheel.

KING PONG.

Dad slams the brakes on. The car lurches forward.

'Get out!' he says.

'But it's not my fault,' I say. 'It was the fly.'

'I don't care whose fault it was,' he says. 'Out!'

'But look!'

I open my hand to show Dad the fly and prove that I'm not lying, but my hand is empty. It must have swerved at the last minute. Outsmarted by a fly! I hate that.

'Out,' says Dad.

Surely he can't be serious.

ELECTRIC CAR.

'I'm sorry, Dad . . . I was just trying to get the fly out of the car . . . in case it caused an accident . . .'

'You're the only one who is going to cause an accident,' he says. 'Out.'

'Mum?' I say. 'Are you going to let him do this?'

I could be the new Michelle Flyffer!

7

'It's for your own good,' she says. 'You've got to learn.'

I open the door.

'You'll be sorry,' I say, 'when you come back and find my bones being picked clean by vultures.'

'There are no vultures in Australia.'

'Kookaburras then.'

'Shut the door,' says Dad. 'You're letting the hot air in.'

There's no reasoning with him.

I get out of the car and shut the door slowly.

The wheels of the car spin. I am showered by gravel. I wipe the grit out of my eyes and look for the car. It's gone.

I look down at my shoes. There is a big red bull ant on my toe. I brush it off. Maybe I should try to catch it. I might need it for food.

Nah. I won't have to eat ants. They'll be back. Any second. Five minutes tops. Just enough to give me a scare.

I start walking.

Actually, it's quite nice. Fresh air. Blue sky. Space. No grumpy parents.

Five minutes pass.

Another five minutes.

And another five minutes.

CUNNING PLACES TO BE SICK IN THE CAR
1. The little ashtray thing ↓
2. Down your little brother's neck
3. In your shoe (desperate)
4. In the interior light cover.
5. Just swallow it.

Romeo, Romeo, wherefore art thou, Romeo?

8

Where are they?

I sit down.

I should just lie down and die—that would teach them.

The only trouble is that it could take a while because I'm actually feeling pretty healthy.

I hear a droning sound in the distance.

Ha! I check my watch. It took them fifteen minutes to give in and come back and get me. That's really going to teach me a lesson I'll never forget. Not.

But as I listen I notice the drone has a different quality. Throatier. Not the putty-putt-putt sound of Dad's car at all.

It's Bike-man!

I jump up and wave.

He waves back and pulls up alongside me.

He looks even crazier close up. His beard is full of insects. Some of them are still alive.

'Well,' he says, 'if it isn't my little mate. What are you doing out here all by yourself?'

'My parents threw me out of the car,' I say. 'They told me I had to walk.'

'You like bikes?' he says.

'Are you kidding?'

'Hop on then,' he says. 'What's your name?'

'Andy. What's yours?'

Tricks to play on a bikie when he/she is not looking

1. Squirt silicon in their helmet, so it sticks to their head... permanently.

2. Stick potatoes up their exhaust pipes.

3. Fill their tyres up with water.

Don't worry bikies never get annoyed.

DO BIKIES HAVE A SENSE OF HUMOUR?

To be, or not to be? OUCH!

9

'Max. Pleased to meet ya!'

He hands me a helmet.

'Here,' he says. 'Put this on.'

It's just like the one he's wearing.

'Hold on,' he says.

'To what?' I yell, but he doesn't hear me above the chugging of his bike.

He gives it full throttle.

My stomach drops as he accelerates up the road.

I grab him around the waist.

Roaring wind. My whole body shaking and vibrating. I'm freezing. I wish I had more clothes on.

I see Mum and Dad's car in the distance.

'That's them!' I yell into Max's ear.

Max surges forward, the old Harley sucking up the highway like spaghetti.

As we pull closer to the car I signal to Max to blow his horn to let them know I'm here.

He blasts. I wave. But they don't stop. If anything they seem to speed up.

Maybe Dad thinks Max is just trying to hassle him. They probably don't recognise me with a helmet on.

'Max!' I yell. 'Go up next to them. I don't think they realise it's me.'

So, Mr Einstein, a more COMPLEX QUESTION!... would you rather be a passenger in a car driven through space by....

1... a foul smelling, short sighted asthmatic lemur OR

2... a mad middle aged mongoose with loose dentures.

That's a hard one, Jana.

I'm going to sneeze.

10

TURN
THE
PAGE
QUICKLY
TO MAKE
$1,000,000.

Max pulls up alongside them.

I wave.

Dad just looks straight ahead.

'Hey,' I yell. 'Stop!'

No reaction.

I wave both hands.

Dad flicks a nervous glance across at me, but he doesn't show any sign of recognition. Instead he hunches over the wheel and pulls away from us at high speed. Wow! I never knew the car could go so fast. If Dad always drove like that, I wouldn't have so much time to get bored.

Max accepts the challenge. He speeds up, but Dad veers onto the other side of the road to block us. Radical!

But Max knows a few tricks, too.

Max pulls back in and rides up the side of the road that Dad has just vacated.

We're back beside them—on the inside lane this time.

Max turns to me and yells above the roar: 'They're not going to stop! You're going to have to board 'em.'

He's joking.

He's got to be. Either that or he's completely insane.

DANGER
LOW
BRIDGE

Aaah. Ahh
AHHHH
Choooo!!

11

'No way!' I yell. 'I'm staying with you.'

'Stand up,' he says. 'I'll go in as close as I can.'

He's not joking.

He rides right up beside the car and signals for me to stand.

I kneel on the seat. I hold on to Max's shoulders and pull myself up. My legs are shaking.

There's still a huge gap.

'It's too far!' I yell.

Max edges in as close as he dares.

The roof is only a metre away.

My stomach is churning.

I don't want to do this.

I'm too young to die!

I bend down.

'I can't do it,' I yell in Max's ear.

'You have to,' he growls.

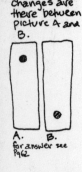
SPOT THE
DIFFERENCE

How many
changes are
there between
picture A and
B.

A.   B.
for answer see
p.162

'Why can't I stay with you?' I say. 'I'll be your apprentice.'

He laughs.

'Highway's no place for a nice kid like you. Go back. Finish school.'

'I'm not nice,' I say. 'I'm really annoying.'

He laughs again, a scary, high-pitched sort of laugh.

'Jump,' he says.

He has a wild look in his eyes. Maybe

staying here is not such a great idea after all.

I stand up again. This is freaky.

I take a deep breath. I close my eyes. Clench my fists. I don't know what good clenching my fists is going to be in this situation—but it feels like the right thing to do.

Goodbye cruel world.

The wind picks me up and sends me hurtling sideways.

Thump!

I land on the car roof. I made it!

Dad starts swerving all over the road. He's trying to shake me off.

I've got to make him realise it's me.

I bang on the roof. Dad swerves harder.

I have an idea.

I edge forward, fingers spread as far apart as they will go.

One mistake and I'm gone.

If I can just let him see it's me he'll slow down.

I push myself down in front of the wind-screen.

Mum and Dad freak. Eyes wide. Mouths open.

FLY OFF
THE
HANDLE.

my head
seems to have
fallen off

WHEN TRAVELLING TO HOLIDAYS WITH A COW ON YOUR ROOF

ALWAYS:

Ⓐ STOP EVERY 2 HOURS TO GIVE THE COW EXERCISE.

Ⓑ STOP EVERY 8 HOURS TO MILK THE COW.

Ⓒ ENGAGE THE COW IN REGULAR CONVERSATION.

Ⓓ FEED IT YOUR LITTLE BROTHER'S CHIPS.

Ⓔ GIVE IT A BLANKET, IT MAY BE FRIESIAN.

Ⓕ

ALLOW IT TO CALL HOME REGULARLY.

Suddenly I go flying forward.

Dad has slammed on the brakes.

I flip over onto my back and grab the aerial to stop myself sliding off the bonnet onto the road.

The car stops.

I'm lying on my back staring up at the sky. Panting hard. It's over.

Mum and Dad get out.

I take off my helmet.

'This is the limit, Andy! The absolute limit!' says Dad. 'What are you trying to do—get yourself killed?'

More dumb questions.

'No,' I say. 'I was trying to get back into the car. You threw me out, remember?'

'Yes,' says Dad. 'To teach you a lesson.'

'What sort of lesson is that?' I say. 'To abandon me in the middle of nowhere with no food, no drink, no map and no sunscreen.'

'We were going to come back,' he says, throwing a glance at Mum. Her cheeks go crimson.

'When?' I say. 'On your way home?'

He looks sheepish.

'We were about to come back and get you when the bikie started chasing us. I was trying

14

to lead him as far away from you as possible. Some of these characters can be pretty dangerous, you know.'

I get into the car.

'I don't want to hear any more excuses, Dad,' I say. 'You tried to get rid of me. You failed. Let's go.'

'We were going to come back,' says Dad. 'Honest.'

He starts the engine. He's feeling bad now. He should be.

We pull out onto the road.

There's an enormous noise outside the car. It's Max. He's riding alongside us. I wind down the window and toss the helmet to him. He catches it with one hand, gives me a big grin and then rockets off into the distance.

I lean back and sigh. Max is cool. Loony, but cool.

Fly fishing

I'm winding the window back up when I see the fly.

It's sitting right on top of Dad's head.

'It's all your fault,' I say quietly. 'I've been abandoned. Almost missed out on my holiday. Risked my life. It's all your fault—and you're going to pay.'

But that's MY job.

15

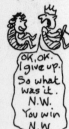

I sit up close behind Dad. I hold my hands just above his head, ready to smash the fly.

It jumps.

The movement distracts me. I clap Dad over both ears instead.

Oops.

His knuckles whiten.

'Dad, I'm sorry—it was a mistake. See, I was trying to . . .'

Dad stops me.

'It's okay, Andy. You don't have to explain.'

'I don't?'

'No. We all make mistakes.'

Oh, I get it. Mum and Dad won't try to put me out of the car again. No matter what I do. They've used their biggest threat and it didn't work. It just made them feel bad.

I sit back in my seat and relax. I close my eyes.

I can do anything now. Anything I want. This might not turn out to be such a boring trip after all. I just have one question.

'Dad?' I say.

'Yes?'

'Are we there yet?'

16

Copycat from Ballarat

My high heels hurt.

My skirt is too long.

My bra is too big.

But I am beautiful.

And, more importantly, I am annoying the hell out of Jen.

I have been copying Jen for two days and she's about ready to kill me.

I have copied her talking. I have copied her walking.

But tonight is the biggest challenge of all.

The school social.

Tonight I'm not only walking and talking like Jen, but I'm dressed like her as well.

We are walking towards the hall. I am

KNOW YOUR BRAS.

1. POINTY ONE

2. OPERA HOUSE MODEL

3. EGYPTIAN TRIPLE

4. GOOD LOOKER

5. BACKPACKER'S SPECIAL.

following a few steps behind her. I swing my arm just like she does. I stick my bum out and sway from side to side. I am doing a brilliant job.

At the foot of the steps she swings around to face me.

I swing around too.

'I don't see you!' she says to my back.

'I don't see you!' I say to nobody.

'I don't hear you,' she says.

'I don't hear you,' I say.

'If you want to make a complete idiot of yourself then fine, go ahead. But the only person you're embarrassing is you. Got it?'

'If you want to make a complete idiot of yourself then fine, go ahead,' I mimic. 'But the only person you're embarrassing is you. Got it?'

She sighs loudly, turns around and stomps up the steps.

I sigh loudly, turn around and stomp up the steps too.

But it's not easy to stomp in high heels. Halfway up I slip and fall back down the stairs. Damn! Jen didn't slip and fall. It's my first mistake of the night.

I'm trying to pick myself up.

18

'Are you alright?' says a deep voice. 'That was a nasty fall.'

Oh no. It's Craig Bennett. Number one school sleaze. The worst thing is that all the girls think he's gorgeous. And doesn't he know it.

He's dressed in a sharp new suit. He reeks of aftershave. He has the top three buttons of his shirt undone. I guess that's so he can show off all three of his chest hairs.

'Here, let me help you,' he says.

Before I can say no he slips his arm around my waist and lifts me up.

He holds me for a second, looking straight into my eyes, before taking his arm away.

What a smooth operator! He makes me want to puke.

'My name's Craig,' he says. 'What's yours?'

'Andy,' I say automatically. Doh! I'm supposed to be a girl!

'Andy?' says Craig.

'I mean Andrea,' I say. 'My friends call me Andy.'

He smiles.

'That's cute. It suits you.'

There's no doubt about it. This guy is good.

CLUNK!!

LEARN
GREAT
DANCE
MOVES

№ 11
The
UMBAWI

'I haven't seen you around before,' he says. 'Are you new?'

'Yes,' I say. 'We've just moved here from Ballarat.'

'Excellent,' says Craig. 'May I escort you in?'

All I want to do is to get away from this creep and go and annoy Jen. But then a thought strikes me. Maybe the best way to annoy Jen is not to copy her, but to enter the social on Craig Bennett's arm. She's as crazy as the rest of the girls about him. When she sees me with him she'll go nuts!

'Yes, that would be . . . elegant,' I say. I think that's what you're supposed to say. I don't know. I've never been in this situation before.

Craig holds out his arm, his elbow bent.

I slip my arm through his and he helps me up the stairs.

Craig opens the door and we walk through.

There's a group of guys hanging around the foyer.

I hear a long low wolf-whistle.

Craig freezes.

He looks in their direction and shakes his head.

Aha! Back in control.

'Kids,' he snorts. 'They're just kids. Ignore them.'

They snigger as we walk past them into the hall.

I look for Jen.

She's standing over near the drinks table with a group of her girlfriends. They are all staring at us. Jen is gaping like a fish. She didn't count on this.

'Would you like a drink?' says Craig.

'Yes thank you,' I say. 'That would be elegant.'

We move towards the table.

White plastic cups are lined up in rows beside a couple of punch bowls.

'Orange or lemon?' says Craig.

'Surprise me,' I say.

Craig picks up two cups and hands one to me. He's about to drink from his cup when I have an idea. I catch hold of his wrist with my free hand and twine my arm around his. We sip our drinks and look deep into each other's eyes. I glance over to make sure Jen is getting all this. She is. She looks furious.

she looked deep into my eyes

She comes over to us.

'Hi, Craig,' she says with the sweetest smile. She's almost as good an actor as I am.

'Hi, Jen,' he replies without taking his eyes off mine.

'Who's your friend?' says Jen.

'Her name's Andrea,' he says. 'She's from Ballarat.'

Buk!

It's time to pluck your eyebrows!

'You can say that again,' says Jen, shooting me a very dirty look.

'Huh?' says Craig. 'Do you two know each other?'

'You could say that,' says Jen.

I shrug.

'Let's dance,' I say. I have to get him away before Jen blows it. I don't want to let her off the hook too soon. I spent hours getting ready—plucking my eyebrows, getting the stupid wig to sit straight, not to mention stuffing my bra with those little white balls from the beanbag. I'm going to make her suffer a while longer.

Is the cup half empty

↓

or half full?

I take Craig's hand and lead him towards the dancefloor, but he doesn't need any encouragement. Craig leaps into the centre of the room and starts going for it like he thinks he's Michael Jackson.

He's pulling every move in the book. Fist in the air. Leg splits. Pirouettes. Even moonwalking. Doesn't this guy have any shame?

wow! Writing!

'Come on,' he says. 'What are you waiting for? Get down! Woooh!'

He shook his head in disbelief.

The only move I'm capable of right at the moment is to shake my head in disbelief. But head-shaking is not exactly a snappy dance move. If I want to keep Craig interested then I'm going to have to get down and dirty—and pretty damn fast.

Trouble is I don't know how.

I've never actually danced before.

I usually spend school socials on the side-lines laughing at everybody else trying to dance.

I don't know the first thing about it.

And then it hits me.

SORRY, IM JUST ANNOYING!

I may not be good at dancing but I am an expert at copying. All I have to do is copy Craig and I'll be fine.

He bends his knees and punches the air.

I follow. Simple enough.

He does a star-jump, a mid-air twist and then lands on his knees.

I do the same. Only I don't land on my knees—I still haven't got the hang of these high heels. I fall backwards onto my bum.

I hear cheering. A large group has formed around us. How embarrassing. I reckon the

Help!

Hey! No time to read

only person more embarrassed than me at this point must be Jen. But I can't back out now.

I pick myself up off the floor.

Craig is on his knees. He's leaning backwards, staring at the roof, shoulders pumping.

I have no choice but to do the same.

Only I throw in an extra touch of my own.

As I lean back I thrust my chest out and shake.

More cheers.

Craig is impressed.

He helps me up and then pulls me close to him.

'I haven't known you for very long, Andrea,' he says, 'but I feel a real connection to you.'

'That's nice,' I say, trying to pull away from him.

I notice that my dancing has caused some of the beanbag balls to fall out of my bra. They are scattered around my feet.

Craig notices too.

'I see you've brought some snow with you from Ballarat!'

I giggle girlishly. 'Oh, Craig. You're so funny. Would you excuse me while I freshen up?'

'Sure,' he says, frowning a little.

SOMETHING TO WEAR TO AVOID BRINGING ATTENTION TO YOURSELF AT A PARTY.

SOME CONVERSATION STARTERS FOR YOUR NEXT PARTY

Hi, I'm A MANIC DEPRESSIVE

I love horses. Are you a horse?

THE BUILDING'S ON FIRE!

24

Time for neck exercises.

He releases his grip on me. I practically run to the toilets at the far end of the hall.

This will not only give me time to repack my bra, but more importantly, give him a bit of time to cool off.

MR.
SCRIBBLE
IN THE
GENTS.

I push open the door of the Mens.

'Hey! You can't go in there,' says a teacher on duty.

Doh! I didn't even think. I'm a girl now. I have to use the Ladies. No way. It must be crawling with girl germs.

I look behind me.

Craig is still standing in the middle of the dancefloor watching me.

I have to go in.

I push open the door. I'm almost knocked backwards by the smell of perfume and hair-spray.

A group of girls are all gathered around the mirror.

'Did you see them?' says one.

'Who *is* that girl he's with?'

'I don't know,' says the first. 'But did you see her dancing?!'

They all giggle.

'Craig deserves better than that. He is so good.'

Up...down...up...

25

The door slams shut behind me.

They look up and go quiet.

I duck into the closest cubicle and lock the door.

I didn't think I was that bad. They're jealous, that's all.

I take my top off and pull my bra straps back onto my shoulder.

More beanbag balls have fallen out of one side than the other. I have to balance them up. I may not be a real girl, but I have my pride.

I hear the group of girls whisper and giggle and then leave the room.

It's safe to come out.

I'm at the basin washing my hands when Lisa Mackney walks in.

She looks even more beautiful than usual. She is so nice. I hope she doesn't recognise me.

I stare down into the basin and pretend not to see her.

'Hi,' she says. 'You're new aren't you? My name's Lisa.'

'Hi, Lisa,' I say. 'I'm Andrea.'

'I know,' she says. 'Everybody's talking about you.'

'Oh?' I say.

Things to fill your bra with.

1. WARM CUSTARD

2.

Lightweight BRICKS

3.

small RODENTS

4

A truck load of GARDEN MULCH.

26

'Yes,' she says. 'You're a really . . . original dancer.'

'Thanks,' I say. 'But it's hard to dance badly when you're with someone as good as Craig.'

Lisa puts her hand on my arm and lowers her voice.

'You musn't take this the wrong way,' she says, 'but just be careful. Craig's got a . . . reputation. I wouldn't want you to get hurt.'

'Thanks,' I say. 'But it's okay. I can look after myself.'

Lisa smiles.

She lowered her voice

She is so beautiful. If there was one girl I could go out with in the whole school it would be her.

But she would never bother with anyone like me. Not dressed like this, anyway.

I become aware that I'm staring at her.

'Are you okay?' she says.

'I'm fine,' I say. 'Just a bit dizzy from the dancing.'

'You remind me of someone,' she says, studying my face.

'Oh really?' I say, starting to panic.

'Yeah,' she says. 'This boy I really like. His name is Andy.'

Arrrh! GASP!

OH, OH.

27

She's blushing. My heart is pounding. Could it be? Nah. Of course not. Could it?

'Andy?' I say. 'Does he have a sister called Jen?'

'Yes!' she says. 'How do you know that?'

'Friends of the family,' I say.

'Really!' she says. 'So you know Andy?'

'Of course,' I say. 'He's a really cool guy.'

'Yes,' says Lisa. 'But he can be very immature at times.'

'Oh!' I say. 'He strikes me as being very mature actually. And *so* good looking!'

'Yes,' says Lisa, sighing. 'I was hoping he would be here tonight.'

'Maybe he'll be here later,' I say.

I can't believe what I'm hearing! If only I wasn't dressed up like a girl I could ask her to dance. I have to get home and change before it's too late.

Lisa shrugs. 'Maybe.'

I dry my sweaty hands on a piece of paper towel.

'I have to get back to the dance,' I say. 'It was nice to meet you.'

'You too,' she says. 'I hope we can be really good friends.'

'Me too,' I say.

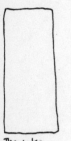

The joke that was placed here last friday, has been removed by person, or persons, unknown. Could they please return it by 5.00 today or face the consequences. Pranks like this are JUST ANNOYING.

'And remember what I said about Craig.'

'Thanks,' I say. 'I'll be careful.'

I pull open the door and go back out into the hall.

I can't see Craig anywhere. Fantastic.

I just want to get home, get changed and get back as quickly as I can.

I'm heading towards the exit when I feel a hand on my shoulder.

MR. SCRIBBLE GOES SURFING

'Hey,' says Craig. 'Where are you going?'

'I have to go home,' I say.

'But it's so early,' he says. 'How about one more dance? You really set that floor alight, you know.'

Dancing with Craig is the last thing I want to do.

she really set the floor alight.

'I've got a big day tomorrow,' I say.

'But it's Saturday. You can sleep in.'

'I have to wash my hair.'

'Just one more,' he begs.

I get the feeling it's going to be quicker to have the dance than to argue.

'One more,' I say, 'and then I really have to go.'

He leads me onto the floor. But this time he doesn't go crazy. He puts his hands

around my waist and tries to pull me towards him.

I try to pull away but he is strong.

The smell of his aftershave is making me feel sick as we shuffle around the floor.

As we pass the drinks table I catch Jen's eye. Help me, I mouth silently. She winks at me. She's enjoying this.

The song finishes.

I pull away from Craig.

'I really have to go now,' I say.

Danny comes up to me. He's the last person I want to see.

'May I have this dance?' he asks.

'In your dreams, buddy,' says Craig, pushing him away and grabbing me around the waist. 'This one's mine.'

'No, it's not,' I say, jerking out of his grasp.

For a moment Craig is stunned. He is not used to being rejected.

He grabs my shoulder.

This speech balloon and shadow is all that remains of a now extinct joke.

I shrug his hand off.

'Stop it!' I say, turning towards the door.

He reaches out to pull me back. I'm quick. But not quick enough.

Craig grabs the back of my dress.

30

The dress rips right down to my waist, revealing my underpants.

I guess you've probably never had the experience of standing in your sister's bra and your Action Man undies in front of the whole school.

If you have, then I feel very sorry for you. If you haven't, then I don't recommend it.

But my embarrassment doesn't end there.

Without the dress to support it, my bra collapses.

The floor is awash with polystyrene balls.

I try to make a run for the door but I trip on my high heels.

Craig reaches forward to stop me falling. He grabs a handful of my hair. My wig comes off in his hand.

'I knew it was you,' says Danny. 'I knew it all along.'

Craig looks at Danny.

Craig looks at me.

He looks at the wig in his hand.

I start to slide away on my back.

'No hard feelings, Craig?' I say. 'Just a bit of fun.'

He throws the wig on the floor.

THE TOP HALF OF THIS REALLY FUNNY DRAWING HAS BEEN REMOVED FOR REPAIRS. (we apologize for just being ANNOYING!)

TRY THIS MAGIC EYE PUZZLE

A pile of scribble

That was frightening.

31

How
TO
BE A
DOG!

1. Look enthusiastic

2. When in doubt, LICK

3. Don't get too close to other dogs.

4. JUST DON'T!

(Sniff)

'I'm going to punch your head in,' he says.

Craig takes off his jacket and starts rolling up his sleeves as he walks towards me.

Jen runs forward. She grabs his arm.

'Don't do that,' she says. 'He's not worth it! He's just a kid. Come and have a drink.'

He looks at me. He looks at Jen. He looks back at me with such anger in his eyes that I wonder if he'll ever get over it.

'Come on,' says Jen.

He turns and allows her to lead him away to the drinks table, his arm around her waist.

I think he'll get over it.

'I knew it was you,' says Danny. 'I wasn't fooled for a second. I just asked you to dance for a laugh.'

I look up.

Lisa Mackney is looking down at me.

'I can explain,' I say.

'Go ahead,' she says.

'Um . . . er . . . I . . . ah . . . um . . .'

'You could always try telling the truth,' she suggests.

She's right. I never thought of that.

'Um—the truth is that I'm very immature for my age.'

Page 32. Only a 1/3 of the way through this book!

'I know,' she says. 'And you know what else?'

'What?' I say.

'You have terrible taste in underpants.'

Terrible taste in Underwear.

Wish you weren't here

I put my suitcase on top of the bed, flick the locks open and lift up the lid.

He's lying there. Staring. He never stops. He's been staring at me day and night since I took him from Mrs Scott's garden a few days ago.

Hands on hips. Little fat belly sticking out of his shirt. And the strangest expression on his face. It could be a smile. It could be a grimace. It's hard to tell.

All I know is that he's not like the other gnomes.

Each year when I come to Mildura to visit my grandparents I borrow one of the gnomes from Mrs Scott's garden and bring it with me. I take a photograph of the gnome and send it to Mrs Scott with a little message on the back saying, 'Having a great time! Wish you were here. Love, Gnome.'

When I get home from the holiday I put the gnome back in her garden—exactly where it was before—and leave Mrs Scott to figure out how on earth a garden gnome manages to travel five hundred kilometres north all by itself.

Sometimes I give them to Danny and other friends to take away as well. In a good year Mrs Scott's gnomes send her postcards from all around Australia.

I don't just do it for Mrs Scott's benefit, though. I also do it because I think it's a nice thing to do for the gnomes. It must be pretty boring just standing in the same spot in the same garden day after day.

They've always looked pretty happy to escape. Until now.

I take the gnome out of the case and lay him on the bed. I rummage through my clothes to find my shorts. I undo the top button of my jeans and unzip my fly. I stop. The gnome is still staring. I turn him over so that he's face down on the bed.

I know it's stupid to be embarrassed about getting changed in front of a concrete gnome

I'm a CHOOK!

but it just doesn't feel right—not the way this gnome stares.

A loud whining noise comes from the backyard.

I go outside.

Grandpa is standing next to what looks like a mini rocket launcher.

'Hey, Andy!' he calls. 'Come and see my new mulcher.'

Every time I visit, Grandpa's got some new garden machine or gadget. His shed looks like a garden supplies warehouse.

'It can chew anything,' he says. 'Watch!'

He picks up a branch thicker than his arm. He flicks the switch and the engine roars into action. Grandpa shoves the branch into the blades. There's a high-pitched whining noise. An explosion of sawdust from the exit chute. No more branch.

'Isn't she great?' says Grandpa. His red face is beaming with pride. 'Want a try?'

'Yeah,' I say.

He hands me a branch. Grey, knotty and gnarled. I jab the end into the blades. It makes a slight whining noise. I pull back.

'Don't be shy,' says Grandpa. 'Push like you mean it.'

I push the branch in hard. Whine, spit, puff! Gone.

'Want to do another?' he says, beaming.

'Yeah,' I say.

Grandpa hands me another branch. I push it in. Gone! He hands me another. Gone! And another. Gone!

Granny sticks her head out of the window.

'There'll be nothing left in the backyard if you carry on at that rate,' she says. 'Why don't you go to the pool, Andy?'

It's not a bad idea. Grandpa's mulcher is fun, but it's hot work.

'Okay, Gran,' I say. 'Can we do some more later, Grandpa?'

'Yes,' he chuckles. 'I'll cut down another tree. That should keep us going.'

I go back to my bedroom to get my towel. The gnome is lying on top of the bed.

But not face down like I left him. He's face up. Staring.

That's weird.

But hang on. My case, which was open, has been closed and placed neatly at the foot of the bed. Granny must have come into the room while I was outside and straightened things up.

But the gnome is starting to freak me out.

WIN FABULOUS PRIZES.

500 PRIZES To Be WON!

Count how many times the PAGE NUMBER FLY claims to be a CHOOK. Check the whole book... then write the number on the back of a SSAE (stamped self addressed envelope)... then POST it, together with your headsize to:

see pg 73.

DO IT NOW.

I'm a fly.

37

I'm going to take the photograph, then wrap him up and try to forget about him so that I can enjoy the rest of my holiday.

I grab my boardshorts, my camera, the gnome and head for the pool.

THERE'S HEAPS OF PEOPLE AT THE SWIMMING POOL.

There's heaps of people at the swimming pool.

The diving tower is working overtime. Dives, bombs, bellywhacks, screams . . .

Hey! I could set the gnome up on the edge of one of the diving boards. It would make a cool photo.

I wonder if it's against the pool rules?

The WORLD'S BEST ANNOYING TRICK... Had to be moved to Pg 60. We apologize for the inconvenience

There's a sign forbidding everything else: no running, no jumping, no horseplay. It doesn't say anything about gnomes, though.

I join the top tower ladder queue. I'm holding the gnome in one hand and have my camera over my shoulder.

I hear laughter behind me. I turn around.

Two big guys are smirking.

'Got your gnome, have ya?'

They crack up laughing.

'Yeah,' I say.

'Or is it your little brother?' says one.

I'm a fly

'Nah, couldn't be,' says the other. 'It's too good looking.'

This cracks them up again. I ignore them. I put my hand on the thin steel of the ladder and pull myself up. My hand is shaking.

I have to admit that I'm not really a top-tower sort of guy. I'm more of a bottom-runger. I usually just put my foot on the first step of the ladder and then take it off again and go and play in the toddlers' pool. I don't really cope with heights very well. But the smirking guys are behind me. I can't back out now. And besides, I want that photograph.

My knuckles whiten as I climb. My knees feel weak, like they'll cave in if I put too much pressure on them.

Finally I reach the platform. It's so high I can practically see the whole town.

The girl in front of me runs along the plank and then pin drops to the water below. She screams the whole way down. It's horrible.

Now it's just me and the smirkers.

'Can you give me a second?' I say. 'I need to take a picture.'

I tiptoe out as far along the plank as I dare. I feel sick. I set the gnome up on the end. It's facing back towards the tower.

BELL

WARNING DO NOT PRESS THIS BELL.

It is wired up to ANDY's earlobes and you may send a 4000V. wake up call to him. SO JUST DON'T DO IT.

You must have been a beautiful maggot.

I'm a CHOOK 39

for those who always open a book at pg 39 and start reading, don't be fooled. The PAGE NUMBER FLY wants you to think he's a chook, but he isn't. OK?

INTRODUCING
NOVELTY
GNOMES

PUNK
GNOME

HAIRY
GNOME

POST
MODERN
GNOME

BUDGET
GNOME

GNOME
SWEET
GNOME.

I return to the platform. I kneel down and point my camera at the gnome. I can hardly hold the camera still enough to take the photo.

'Smile,' says one of the smirkers.

'He looks like he's in pain,' says the other.

'Maybe his pants are too tight.'

They crack up laughing again. Maybe *their* pants are too tight.

I take a few shots and tiptoe back out onto the plank to retrieve my gnome. I crouch down to pick him up. I'm trying not to look at the pool below in case I get any more dizzy than I already am. I place my hand on his hat. As I stand up he seems to jump.

I lose my balance and slip. I grab the end of the diving board. I'm hanging by one hand. The gnome has fallen over onto his side. His head is sticking over the edge of the board. Staring at me. But it's not a look of pain on his face any more. That's a smile.

I'm slipping. I'm only holding on by two fingers.

Oops.

Make that one finger.

I can't hold on any more. I'm falling. I hit the water belly first. But I'm alive. I push my

FLY!

40

way back up to the surface. Spitting and choking.

I look back up at the board.

The gnome is plummeting towards me. He's not content with making me fall, now he's trying to knock me out. He wants to drown me.

WHOOOMP!

The gnome does a fantastic pin drop into the centre of the pool and sinks straight to the bottom.

A woman starts screaming and pointing at me.

'Guard! A small child has fallen into the pool!'

'I'm not that small,' I call.

The guard dives into the pool. But he doesn't try to save me. He dives down to the bottom of the pool and emerges with the gnome in his hand.

He is not happy.

'Is this yours?' he says.

'Yes,' I say.

'Would you mind explaining what he's doing in here?'

'Swimming?' I say.

'Do you realise that garden gnomes are banned from the pool?' he says.

WIN FABULOUS PRIZES! (continued from Pg 73) ...A FROZEN CHICKEN CAR.

Yes, it's your lucky day. The Frozen CHICKEN CAR (FCC) is yours. A choice of 3 colours (white, black or Rhode Is. red) 2 models (Roaster or boiler). 2nd with or without chips. BUK BUK

Fly! I'm a FLY!

41

MUM.

SWIMMING
POOL
GNOME.

'It doesn't say that on the sign,' I say.

'It shouldn't have to,' he says. 'It should be obvious.'

He hands it back to me.

'Get rid of it.'

The smirkers are laughing as I leave.

Maybe this whole thing was their fault. Maybe I fell off the board because they bounced on it while I was trying to get the gnome. Maybe it was them who kicked it off afterwards. Maybe I'm just being paranoid.

Maybe.

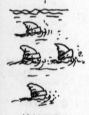

KILLER
GNOMES

I'm lying in bed.

The night is still and hot.

I can't sleep.

I hear the high-pitched whine of an approaching mosquito. I wait until it gets really loud. It stops. I can feel it on my fore-head. I bring my hand up slowly. I whack my head with my open palm. The whining starts up again as the mosquito retreats to the roof. Just like the other forty times.

I can't stop thinking about the gnome.

Before I went to bed I wrapped him in a plastic bag and fastened it with fat rubber bands. I buried him down the bottom of my case under all my clothes. I locked the case and pushed it under the bed.

He would have to be Houdini to get out of there.

But I'm still scared.

He tried to kill me this afternoon. I think. In fact I'm positive. Sort of.

I hear a noise.

It sounds like somebody knocking.

'Come in,' I call.

But nobody comes.

I hear the knocking again. I get out of bed and open the door. Nobody there. Am I going mad?

I get back into bed.

More knocking.

It's not the door at all.

It's coming from under the bed.

I hear the locks of the suitcase click open.

I can't believe it.

This is crazy.

A concrete garden gnome wrapped in plastic secured by fat rubber bands cannot open a suitcase. Especially not from the inside.

I close my eyes and try to go back to sleep.

NAUGHTY GNOMES HOW TO DISCIPLINE THEM.

1. Speak to them firmly.

2. Slap them on the nose.

3. If the behaviour is repeated, then speak to them VERY firmly.

4. If the behaviour is repeated insert gnome in compost bin.

5. Buy new gnome.

But I can't sleep.

I hear rustling.

This is ridiculous.

I grab my torch and jump out of bed. I shine the torch under the bed at my case. It's locked. I knew I was imagining it. I just had to check.

I switch off the torch and get back into bed.

I turn onto my side and try to relax.

I'm just on the edge of falling asleep when I hear the mosquito.

I swipe at it. Miss. It returns. I swipe again. The back of my hand hits something hard under the sheet. I pull the sheet back. It's the gnome. Lying on his side. Staring at me.

I grab him and throw him against the wall with super-human strength.

The gnome bounces off the wall and lands back on the bed.

I pick him up again and throw him even harder.

This time he doesn't return.

I grab my torch and shine it at the floor.

The gnome is broken in two. His head has come off his body. I pick up the two pieces. I take them to the back door and throw them as far away from the house as I can.

I go back to bed.

The nightmare is over.

"Ave there any stories about mechanical gnomes in this book?" it said

The next morning I get up and go to the kitchen.

Grandpa is sitting at the kitchen table with his back to me.

'Morning, Grandpa,' I call.

'Good morning, Andy,' he says. 'I found your friend in the backyard.'

'Huh?' I say.

Grandpa turns around.

"There'd better not be," whispered the mechanical bird.

In his hand is the gnome. He has glued the head back onto the body.

A huge jagged crack runs from shoulder to shoulder. He looks even uglier than before.

'Gee, thanks, Grandpa.'

'That's alright, son,' he says. Have an accident, did ya?'

'Ah, yeah, you could say that.'

'You must be really attached to that gnome,' says Grandpa, 'to bring him all this way.'

'Ah, yeah, you could say that, too,' I say.

*

45

It's late afternoon. Grandma and Grandpa have gone out. I'm home alone. This is the moment I've been waiting for.

I pick up the gnome by his hat, hold him at arm's length and take him out to the backyard.

I've got a little job for Grandpa's mulcher.

I flick the switch. The engine roars. The mulcher is hungry—ready for action.

I pause.

ELECTED BY A QUIRK OF THE ELECTORAL SYSTEM, The new Prime Minister BACK-GARDEN GNOME prepares to meet the press.

What am I doing?! I am about to throw a garden gnome into a garden mulcher. The gnome is not smiling now. He's looking up at me with big pleading eyes like an innocent child. But this is just part of his evil magic. He is not a child. And he is definitely not innocent.

I push him into the mulcher.

More tree limbs.

He flies straight back out. The gnome is lying on the ground grinning at me. His two painted eyes are cold and black.

There is no doubt. The gnome is a killer. It's either him or me. I pick him up again.

'Say your prayers,' I tell him.

I drop him into the top and use a tree branch to force him into the blades.

The blades whine. Or is that the gnome screaming?

The mulcher coughs out an enormous wad of dust and propels coloured shrapnel into the air.

I flick the switch off.

All is silent.

I lean on the mulcher. Panting. Waiting. Half expecting the gnome dust to reassemble itself and come at me.

But nothing happens.

I have saved the world from the evil gnome. Not that anybody will ever know. I hate that. You do this brave heroic thing and you can't tell anybody because if you do they'll think you're crazy.

I go back inside.

Grandma and Grandpa are home.

'Are you feeling alright?' says Granny. 'You look a bit pale.'

'I'm okay,' I say. 'Just a bit tired—I'm going to lie down.'

I push open the door of my bedroom.

I scream.

The gnome is lying on top of the bed.

↓

SPINY
ANT
EATER

↓

GLUE
TONGUED
LIZARD.

Staring straight at me. Grinning. He *has* reassembled himself. Payback time. The room starts spinning and I fall to the floor.

Grandma and Grandpa rush in.

'Andy!' says Granny. 'What's the matter?'

I'm trying to tell them, but nothing is coming out. I just open and shut my mouth like a fish out of water. I point at the gnome. My hand is shaking.

'The gnome,' I whisper. 'The gnome . . .'

'Do you like it?' says Grandpa, helping me up. 'We found it at the market. It's exactly the same as your other one—only without a broken neck. Thought it might cheer you up.'

'It's not the same gnome?'

'No, of course not,' says Granny. 'But it's almost identical. We thought you'd like it.'

'I do! I do!' I say. 'I love it!'

I pick it up, cuddle it and give it a big kiss.

Granny and Grandpa smile, pleased with their work. They leave.

I place the gnome back on the bed. I'm not taking my eyes off him for a moment. But nothing happens.

I kneel down and put my face close to his.

'Any funny stuff and it's Grandpa's mulcher . . . just like your friend. Got it?'

The gnome just stares.

And smiles.

Well, it could be a smile. It could be a grimace. It's hard to tell.

INTERESTING
GARDEN
SCULPTURES.

49

Imaginary friends

A drawing by my friend the imaginary illustrator.

omorrow is our school sports carnival. I don't want to go. Not because I'm not good at sport. I can run faster, jump higher and throw stuff further than anybody in the school, but I don't like to do it. It would be boring with me just winning everything all day long. I like to give the other kids a chance. That's just the sort of thoughtful person I am.

But try telling that to my Mum. She has this crazy idea that I don't like sport and that I try to get out of it whenever I can.

That's why I've brought Fred home. Fred's my imaginary friend. I'm going to tell Mum he's sick and that I have to stay home from school to look after him. It can't fail. Either

she'll think that I'm going crazy and keep me home from school, or she'll be sucked in and let me stay home to look after Fred. I can't lose.

I open the back door and drop my bag on the laundry floor.

'Mum?' I call.

'I'm in here,' she says.

I find her in the kitchen. She's chopping onions.

'Mum, I'd like you to meet a friend of mine. His name is Fred.'

'But there's nobody there,' says Mum.

'Don't be like that,' I say. 'You'll hurt his feelings.'

Mum frowns.

'Are you feeling alright?'

'Who are you asking,' I say. 'Me or Fred?'

'You,' she says.

'I'm fine,' I say. 'It's Fred who is not feeling so good. He's got a stomach ache. He wants to know if I can stay home from school tomorrow to look after him.'

I pretend to help Fred over to a chair. I go to the sink, run a sponge under cold water and then mop Fred's brow with it. Mum is watching me with a frown.

FAMOUS PAINTINGS # 12.

LEONAROO DA CHOOKI'S MONA LISA.

Gday Hello 51

'I think he's running a temperature,' I explain. 'I don't want to miss out on the school sports carnival, but I really think I should stay home and look after him.'

'What about his parents?' says Mum.

'They've gone on an overseas holiday.'

'And left him all alone?'

'They didn't want him to miss out on any school.'

'I could look after him,' says Mum.

'Don't be silly, Mum—you've got plenty to do without having to look after Fred as well.'

'No, it would be a pleasure,' says Mum. 'Your friends are very important to me.'

'Fred is very important to me, too,' I say. 'I wouldn't feel right leaving him.'

'But I know how much the sports carnival means to you,' says Mum.

'Yes, but I couldn't enjoy the carnival knowing Fred is home sick. If he gets any worse overnight, I'll have to stay home.'

'I really don't think that will be necessary,' says Mum. 'I *am* a trained nurse. I think the best thing you could do for Fred would be to go out there tomorrow and just do your best. Make him proud of you.'

'Maybe,' I say, 'assuming that he lives long enough to hear the results.'

Gee, I wish I could find a girlfriend with interesting ears.

(This picture should be on Pg 242)

'Dinner's ready,' calls Mum.

I walk into the kitchen.

Mum has set three places. But there's only two of us. Jen is away on a school camp and Dad is on a work trip.

'Who's coming to dinner, Mum?'

She gives me a strange look.

'Why, Fred of course.'

'Oh yeah,' I say. 'Of course.'

'Well,' says Mum. 'Don't just make him stand there. Invite him to sit down.'

'Have a seat, Fred,' I say.

Mum motions to me to pull the chair out for him.

We both know this is completely stupid, but to not do it would be to admit that Fred is not real. And that means the sports carnival for sure.

I walk around to the chair against the wall. I pull it out and bow low.

'Your chair, Monsieur Fred,' I say.

I give him time to sit down and then I push his chair in.

Politician with Integrity by Hans. R. Loos.

A shadow of its former self.

Who's me?

I am me.

53

(This joke should be on page 242)

Mum places a heaped plate of steaming casserole in front of Fred.

'There you are,' she says. 'I know you're probably not hungry, but try to eat as much as you can. You need to keep your strength up when you're as sick as you are.'

My mouth is watering. I'm so hungry.

Mum places a plate in front of me. But it's not as generous as Fred's serve. In fact it's hardly enough for a mouse.

'Is there a food shortage?' I say.

'There is tonight,' she says. 'I didn't plan for an extra guest. You'll have to share your dinner with Fred.'

'But he's getting more than me.'

'He's sick! Don't you want him to get better?'

'Well of course I do, but . . .'

'But what?'

'It's no use him getting better if I starve to death.'

'Andy,' says Mum, 'I must say I'm a little shocked at your selfishness. Fred is a very sick boy. We have to do everything we can to help him.'

'Yes, Mum.'

I eat my dinner in about three seconds flat.

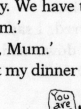

54

Fred, of course, doesn't touch his.

At the end of the meal Mum starts collecting the plates.

'What's going to happen to Fred's dinner?' I say.

'I'll put it in the fridge. He might want it tomorrow.'

'And if he doesn't want it can I have it?'

'No, I don't think that would be a good idea,' says Mum. 'He's probably put his germs all over it. I don't want you getting sick as well.'

Mum picks up his plate and stretches a sheet of Glad Wrap across it.

'Well,' she says, 'what are you waiting for? Go and set up the camp bed for Fred. I expect he'll be wanting an early night, poor thing.'

'Can't he sleep in Jen's room?'

'But he's *your* friend. Besides, I think someone should be with him. In case he gets sick during the night.'

I go to the hall cupboard to get the bed. I have to unpack about a billion other pieces of junk to get to it. Old surfboards, Dad's golf buggy, a totem tennis set, boxes of Christmas decorations and a huge red esky have to be removed before I can reach the bed.

55

I drag it out. Looks like it was the original camp bed made before they'd worked out how to make them properly. It weighs about seventeen tonnes. Its springs are all sticking out at crazy angles. I lug the beast down the hallway. One of the springs catches on my windcheater. I start to unpick it. A daddy longlegs appears from the top of the mattress. It's right in front of my eyes. I get such a fright that I drop the bed. It falls onto my foot. A perfect five-toe crush.

'FRUIT TINGLES!' I scream.

'Andy!' says Mum from the living room. 'Language! We have a guest, remember?'

How could I forget? I've got five toes' worth of throbbing pain to remind me.

I drag the camp bed the rest of the way up the hall and into my bedroom. I wrestle with the catch. The bed springs open with lethal force.

THE CAMP BED STRIKES BACK.

I go to the linen cupboard and get sheets, blankets and a pillow.

I bring them back and start making the bed. If there's one thing I hate it's making beds. I can never get them smooth. There's always this stupid ripple running from one corner to the other. Someone should invent spray-on sheets. They would make a fortune.

But you can't be me.

After about five hours I finish the bed. I come back to the loungeroom.

Tonight it's *The Simpsons*. I've been looking forward to watching it all day. But Mum is watching some stupid documentary about the economy.

'Mum, can we watch *The Simpsons*?'

'Well, I wouldn't mind,' she says, 'but Fred said he prefers documentaries . . . he's very intellectual, you know.'

'Very funny, Mum,' I say. This has gone far enough. I don't care about the sports carnival any more. I just want to watch *The Simpsons*.

'I surrender,' I say. 'You win, okay?'

'What do you mean?' says Mum.

'There's no such person as Fred!'

'Andy,' says Mum. 'You'll hurt Fred's feelings.'

'But he doesn't have any feelings. He doesn't exist!'

The new Prime Minister, Mr Camp Bed, speaks to the public.

'Andy, that is a horrible thing to say. How would you like it if Fred said you didn't exist?'

'That would be a laugh. Somebody who doesn't exist telling somebody who does exist that they don't exist.'

'That's it. Fred and I have had enough of your rudeness. Go to your room.'

BEWARE OF CAMP BEDS HIDING IN PUBLIC PLACES.

I'm home from the sports carnival. I can hardly walk. My legs are aching. And I didn't win a single ribbon. Not that I tried, of course. I had to let the others have a go.

The house is empty. The lights are off. Mum is out.

I'm in the kitchen spooning honey over a bowl of Vita Brits when the front door opens.

I can hear Mum talking and laughing.

She comes into the kitchen. She is holding a stick of fairy floss.

'Where have you been?' I ask.

'At the zoo,' she says.

'Why didn't you take me?'

'Well, I know how much the sports carnival means to you. Besides, I wanted to do something special for Fred.'

I pound my fist on the table. 'Fred's my imaginary friend,' I yell, 'not yours. You've got no right to take him to the zoo without me.'

'Come now, Andy,' says Mum. 'Fred's had

Because I'm me

a pretty miserable time of it. We have to make allowances.'

I look at the fresh stick of fairy floss in her hand. Pink, shiny and fluffy. Perfect.

'Is that for me?' I ask.

'No,' says Mum. 'It's Fred's.'

'Can I have some?'

'Well, I don't know. You'll have to ask Fred.'

I feel really dumb asking an imaginary person for fairy floss, but I'm desperate. Mum never buys fairy floss for me.

'Fred,' I say to the blank space where Fred is supposed to be standing, 'may I please have some of your fairy floss?'

We both look at the blank space.

I can't hear anything, but Mum is nodding intently.

She turns to me.

'He says he'd prefer not to share it with you, because he's worried that you'll get his disease.'

'It's not fair. Why does Fred get fairy floss and I don't?'

'Because it rots your teeth.'

'What about Fred's teeth?' I say.

'He's sick. Surely you wouldn't begrudge him this little pleasure, would you?'

Mr. Scribble and his angry wife.

Mrs CAMP BED COMPETES IN THE SKI JUMP AT THE WINTER OLYMPICS. (Unsuccessfully, she folded after the first round)

We must be related.

59

I give up. I might as well try bashing down a brick wall with my head. Mum's not going to budge.

'Andy,' says Mum, 'would you mind sleeping in the camp bed tonight? Fred's had such a big day at the zoo. I think he needs the comfort of a proper bed. Would you mind? Please? He is our guest.'

'Yeah right, Mum,' I say. 'And would you like me to sit by his bed and hold a bucket for him to sick up all his fairy floss into as well?'

Mum looks shocked.

'There's no need to talk like that, Andy.'

'Get it into your head, Mum—there is no Fred!'

'I'm sorry, Andy,' says Mum, 'but this is no way to treat a guest. Please go to your room right now, and don't come out until you can be civil.'

I go to my room. I would stomp except my legs are aching and my crushed toes are still hurting. I have to do a sort of angry limp instead.

I wish I'd never invented Fred. He's stolen my dinner, my television show, my trip to the zoo—even my mother. And now he wants my bed. Well, forget it. Fred has to go. There's

You don't even exist.

60

not enough room in the house for both of us.

But how do you get rid of someone who doesn't exist in the first place?

I've got it. You invent somebody else who doesn't exist to get rid of them for you.

I need an imaginary friend who's not going to turn out to be a mummy's boy like Fred. He's got to be bad. Superbad. His name is going to be Damien. He doesn't wash his hands after going to the toilet. He doesn't say please and he doesn't say thank you. He wears his baseball cap backwards and goes swimming in heavy surf less than half an hour after big meals. He sticks forks in toasters—just for the fun of it. He doesn't talk about his problems—he solves them with violence, and plenty of it. He hates vegetables. He hates girls. And, most of all, he hates goody-goodies. And tomorrow I will introduce him to Fred.

I'm woken by the sound of Mum's laughter.

I put my dressing gown over my pyjamas and go to the door of the kitchen.

Mum is fussing around Fred's chair.

She sees me standing at the door.

61

'Good morning Andy,' she says. 'Come in and join us.'

'Mum,' I say, 'I'd like you to meet another friend of mine. His name is Damien. His parents are overseas.'

SUN TAN
FOR RATS.

Mum doesn't miss a beat. She comes across to me and mimes a handshake with Damien.

'Pleased to meet you, Damien,' she says. 'Would you like some breakfast?'

'Is that alright, Mum?' I ask. 'I know it's kind of short notice, but . . .'

'Shush, Andy,' says Mum. 'Damien's talking.'

'Sorry,' I say.

Mum stands listening to Damien. She laughs.

ANSWER TO
SPOT THE
DIFFERENCE
Pg 12.
It's a
trick.

A ●   ●B

The pictures
are the
same. In B
the universe
was rotated
through 180°.

'Have a seat,' says Mum, pulling out a chair for Damien. 'Would you like some porridge?'

'Yes,' I say. 'I'm starving.'

Mum glares at me.

'I was talking to Damien.'

She takes his order.

'What a lovely boy,' she says to me as she crosses to the stove. 'And so polite.'

Damien? Polite? But he's not supposed to say please or thank you. And he's supposed to hate girls. That includes mothers. What's wrong with me? Am I losing my touch? Am I

TV
STAR

I
can't
see
you.

62

going soft? Is it really so hard to invent an imaginary friend that my mother won't fall in love with?

'Mum, what about me?' I say. 'Can I have some porridge?'

'There's not much porridge left,' she says. 'But there's a little bit of toast . . . if you don't mind the crusts, that is. Fred doesn't like the crusts so I gave him the rest of the loaf. I hope you don't mind.'

I look at Fred's plate piled high with freshly buttered toast. There's at least ten pieces there.

Mum places two blackened, shrivelled crusts in front of me.

'They got a bit burnt,' she says. 'And I'm afraid there's no butter left, either.'

'Don't tell me,' I say. 'You used it all on Fred's toast.'

'That's right,' says Mum. 'How did you know?'

'Just a hunch,' I say.

The telephone rings. Mum goes into the living room to answer it. Now is my chance.

I sit down in Fred's chair and help myself to his toast.

Mum comes in. She flips.

WOULD YOU RATHER . . . ANSWER from Pg 83.

B was/is the correct answer. 9 out of 10 young adults prefer to wear a pickaxe through their nostrils than any other body part.

It's cool and its unambiguous.

It's you that doesn't exist.

'Andy! What are you doing? That's Fred's breakfast.'

'He had to go,' I say. 'Damien too.'

Mum looks at Damien's chair and then back to mine.

'But I didn't get to say goodbye.'

'I know,' I say. 'They slipped out while you were on the phone.'

'But why?'

I have to think fast.

'Their parents came home early. They said to say thanks and all that. They would have said goodbye themselves but they didn't want to disturb you.'

Mum sits down, shaking her head.

'But I was going to cook Fred's favourite dinner tonight. Cauliflower surprise. He told me he'd be here.'

'Oh well,' I say, 'Fred's a bit like that. Damien too. Nice boys, but very unreliable. When it comes down to it they're both just out for themselves.'

Mum looks like she's about to cry. This is going too far. Dad and Jen have obviously been away too long. I have to snap her out of it. Tell her the truth.

'Listen, Mum,' I say. 'There's something

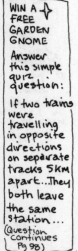

WIN A
FREE
GARDEN
GNOME
Answer
this simple
quiz
question:

If two trains
were
travelling
in opposite
directions
on separate
tracks 5km
apart...They
both leave
the same
station...
(Question
continues
Pg 98)

But
I'm
ME!!

64

you have to understand. Fred and Damien were not real. I made them up.'

'You did?'

'Yes,' I say. 'But I never counted on you getting so attached to them.'

Mum doesn't say anything.

She stares at the table.

I feel like I've just committed a double homicide.

Mrs Smith and her dining room table holidaying on the Gold Coast.

But I think I've finally got through. Sometimes the truth hurts.

I get up and pull out a chair next to hers.

'It's okay, Mum,' I say. 'You've still got me. *I'm* real.' I go to sit down.

Mum screams.

'You can't sit there,' she says. 'It's taken.'

I sigh.

'Mum, I thought we'd got this straight. There is no Fred. There is no Damien. There's just you and me.'

'And Frieda,' says Mum, nodding towards the empty chair.

'Frieda?'

'Yes,' says Mum. 'She'll be staying with us for a few weeks. See, her parents have gone overseas and . . .'

'Don't tell me, Mum,' I say. 'She hates crusts.'

CAULIFLOWER
SURPRISE

'That's right,' says Mum.

'And her favourite meal is cauliflower surprise?'

'Right again,' says Mum, beaming. 'How did you know?'

'Just a hunch,' I say.

SLURP!!!

You've just Annoying.

In the shower
with Andy

I'm in the shower. Singing. And not just because the echo makes my voice sound so cool either. I'm singing because I'm so happy.

Ever since I've been old enough to have showers I've been trying to find a way to fill a shower cubicle up with water. If I put a face-washer over the plughole I can get the water as far up as my ankles, but it always ends up leaking out through the gaps in the door.

But I think I've finally found the answer— Dad's silicone gun.

I've plugged up the plughole.

I've sealed up the shower-screen doors.

I've even filled in all the cracks in the tiles.

In the making of this story no face washers were harmed.

MR. SILICONE

The cubicle is completely watertight and the water is already up to my knees.

And the best thing is that I've got all night to enjoy it.

Mum and Dad have got Mr and Mrs Bainbridge over for dinner. They'll be too busy listening to Mr Bainbridge talking about himself to have time to worry about what I'm doing.

I hear banging on the door.

'Have you almost finished, Andy?'

It's Jen!

'No,' I say. 'I think I'm going to be in here a while yet.'

'Can you hurry up?' yells Jen.

'But you already had your shower this morning,' I yell.

'I'm going out,' she says. 'I need the bathroom!'

'Okay. I'll be out in a minute,' I call. I always say that. It's the truth. Sort of. I will be out in a minute—I'm just not saying which minute it will be.

The cubicle is filling with thick white steam. Just the way I like it. Dad's always telling us how important it is to turn the fan on when we're having a shower, but I can't see

Even the humblest bar of soap can dream of greatness.

68

the point. A shower without steam doesn't make sense. You might as well go and stand outside in the rain.

My rubber duck bumps against my legs. I pick it up.

'This is it,' I say. 'Just you and me . . . going where no boy—or rubber duck—has ever gone before.'

It has its bill raised in a sort of a smile. It must be as excited as I am. Let's face it, there can't be that much excitement in the life of a rubber duck. Except that you'd get to see everybody without their clothes on.

Jen bangs on the door again.

'Andy! Pleeeeease!'

'Okay,' I call. 'I'll be out in a minute.'

'You said that a minute ago.'

'I'm washing my hair.'

'But you've been in there for at least half an hour. You don't have *that* much hair.'

'I'm using a new sort of shampoo—I have to do it strand by strand.'

'Andy!'

The water is almost up to my belly-button. There's only one thing missing. Bubbles!

I pick up the bubblebath and measure out a capful. I tip it into the water. A few bubbles,

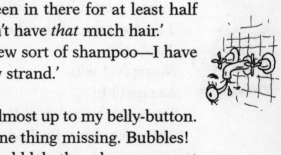

NEW FROM
20th CENTURY
FLOPS
A
MOVIE
WITH
A
DIFFERENCE
BRANDO!
The
NASTY
RUBBER
DUCKY

He chews
ankles,
terrovizes
face washers,
pulls out
bath plugs...
BATH
TIME
WILL
NEVER
BE
THE
SAME.

69

but not enough. I add another cap. And another. And another. One more for good measure. Another for good luck.

I keep adding bubblebath until the bottle is empty. The bubbles rise over my head. Cool. It's like I'm being eaten by this enormous white fungus. Well, not that being eaten by an enormous white fungus would be cool—it would probably be quite uncool, actually—but you know what I mean.

Jen is yelling.

'Andy, if you don't get out right this minute, you're going to be sorry.'

Jen is persistent, I'll give her that. But I'll fix her. I'll use my old 'what did you say?' routine.

'Pardon?' I yell. 'What did you say?'

'I said you're going to be sorry!'

'What? I can't hear you!'

'I said get out of the shower!'

'Pardon?'

No reply. I win.

Aaaagghhh!

The water's gone hot! Boiling hot!

Jen must have flushed the toilet. That's bad news.

I lose.

I jump back against the shower wall.

Hot water splatters onto my face. My chest. My arms.

I grab the cold tap and turn it on full.

The hot water disappears. Now it's freezing.

I'm going to have to turn both taps off and start all over again. I hate that. Being a pioneer is not easy.

BATHROOM DANGERS No 37

BATH SHARKS.

I turn the hot tap off. But the cold won't budge.

I grab the tap with both hands. I try to twist it clockwise but it's stuck. Not even my super-strength can move it.

The silicone gun is hanging off the shower pipe. I pick it up and start bashing the tap with it. That should loosen it.

But the handgrip shatters.

The pieces disappear into the soapy water. I'm staring at a thin metal rod coming out of the wall. And the water is still flowing full blast.

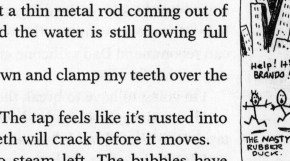
Help! It's BRANDO!

THE NASTY RUBBER DUCK.

I kneel down and clamp my teeth over the tap rod.

No good. The tap feels like it's rusted into place. My teeth will crack before it moves.

There's no steam left. The bubbles have been flattened. The freezing water is almost

Hello little green men

up to my chest. Maybe this wasn't such a great idea.

Time to bail out.

I take a deep breath and dive to the bottom of the shower. I'm trying to find the plughole. I've got to get the silicone out before the shower fills up completely.

But I can't do it. I did the job too well. There's nothing but a hard rubbery slab of silicone where the plug used to be. I can't poke through it. I can't get a fingernail underneath to lift it up. It's times like this I wish I didn't bite my nails. But then it's times like this that cause me to bite my nails in the first place.

I stand up, gasping for air. The water is up to my neck. I grab hold of the doorhandle and try to wrench it open but I laid the silicone even thicker on the doors than the plughole. If you ever want anything sealed tight I can recommend Dad's silicone gun. This stuff stays stuck forever.

I'm going to have to break the door down.

I'll use the gun. It made short work of the tap so the door shouldn't be a problem.

I bash the glass with the gun handle. It bounces off. I bash it again, harder this time.

SHOWER CUBICLE WILDLIFE GUIDE:

DUCK BRUSH

WASHER FISH

LEGO CRUSTACEAN

TOE-NAIL CLIPPING

BELLY-BUTTON FLUFF

SOAP SLIVER

PLUGHOLE KELP.

The gun snaps in two. Just my luck. Reinforced shower screen glass. Unbreakable.

I'm shivering. And not just from the cold. I'm scared.

I start bashing the door with the duck.

'HELP! I'M DROWNING! HELP!'

'I'm not surprised!' Jen yells back. 'You've been in there long enough.'

'Jen, I'm not kidding. Help me!'

'What did you say?' she says. 'I can't hear you.'

'Be serious,' I yell. 'I've siliconed myself in here.'

'What?'

She wins again.

I'm treading water. My head is very close to the top of the shower.

The only way I can save myself is to get rid of the water.

I'm going to have to drink it.

Dirty soapy shower water.

I'd rather die.

The water nudges the tip of my nose.

Actually, on second thoughts I'd rather drink the water.

I start swallowing.

It's working. I just have to drink as fast as

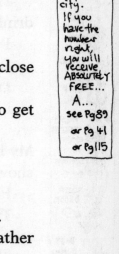

WIN FABULOUS PRIZES!! continued from Pg 37 ... send it to: The Chicken Marketing BOARD P.O Box 100,000,000 in your capital city. If you have the number right, you will receive ABSOLUTELY FREE... A... see Pg89 or Pg 41 or Pg 115

the shower is filling up. And if I can drink even faster then I might get out of here alive yet. Actually the water doesn't taste that bad—it's only been three days since my last shower.

I keep swallowing.

And swallowing. And swallowing. And swallowing.

Uh-oh.

I can't believe this.

I need to go to the toilet.

But I can't.

I'll drink dirty shower water but I won't drink that.

I've got to hold on.

But I can't do that, either.

I'm busting.

My head is bumping against the roof of the shower.

It's getting harder to breathe.

There's more banging on the door but it sounds like it's coming from a long way away.

'I'm going to tell Dad,' says Jen in a distant voice. 'Is that what you want? Is it?'

'Yes Jen,' I call. 'Yes! Please hurry!'

BATHROOM DANGERS.

INNOCENT LOOKING DARK HAIRS STICKING OUT OF PLUGHOLE. BE CAREFUL, THERE IS A COMPLETE LIFE FORM ATTACHED

HAIR

SOAP GLOB

LEGO

GOLF BALL

FALSE TEETH

Mr. Scribble !!!

TOOTH BRUSH

BABY'S DUMMY.

SPUNK!

Everything becomes quiet.

My life is flashing before my eyes.

I see myself blowing a high-pitched whistle while Mum is trying to talk on the telephone. I see myself letting down the tyres on Dad's car. I see myself hiding a rubber snake in Jen's bed. Is that all I did with my life? Annoy people? Surely I did something useful . . . something good?

REMAIN LEVEL HEADED

OR FACE

THE CONSEQUENCES.

Nope. I can't think of anything. Except for solving the problem of how to fill a shower cubicle with water.

I may be going to die, but at least it will be a hero's death. Future generations of Australian children will thank me as they float around in their sealed-up shower cubicles.

FIRST SHOWER CUBICLE IN SPACE

Ouch!

Something is pressing into the top of my head.

I look up.

The fan! I forgot all about it.

It's not very big, but it's better than nothing. If I can get the grille off then I can escape through the hole and up into the roof.

I work my fingers under the edge of the grille and pull on it. It comes off easily.

I reach into the casing and grab hold of the

fan. I rock it back and forth. There is a little bit of give in it. I start giving it all I've got.

Finally the bolts holding it give way. I push my arms and head into the hole, kicking like mad to get the thrust I need to make it all the way up.

The opening is smaller than I thought. I expel every last bit of air in my lungs to make myself thin enough to fit through the hole. Not that there was much air left in them, but it seems to help.

At last! I'm through!

I'm lying on a yellow insulation batt in the roof of our house. The glass fibres are prickly on my skin, but I'm not complaining. It's a lot better than where I was. I look back into the hole. It's like one of those fishing holes that Eskimos cut in the ice. But there's no fish. Just my rubber duck. I reach down and pick it out. We're in this together. I can't just leave it.

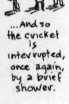

...And so the cricket is interrupted, once again, by a brief shower.

After I get my breath back I look around.

I know there's a manhole in the top of the kitchen. All I have to do is to locate it, climb down into the kitchen and nick down the hallway into my room. Then I can put my pyjamas on and go to bed early. It will save a

SPUNK!

munch munch

lot of boring explanation—and, if I'm really lucky, Jen will get the blame.

I have to move fast. I start crawling towards the kitchen. I'm carrying the duck in one hand and using my other hand to feel my way along the roof beam.

Suddenly I feel a sharp pain in my thumb. I jerk my hand back and almost lose my balance. I fling the duck away so I can grab the beam with my other hand.

I look at my thumb. A huge splinter is sticking out of it. I pull it out with my teeth. Ouch!

I shake my hand a few times and look around for my duck. It has landed in the middle of a large unsupported section of insulation batts. I'm tempted to leave it there. But that wouldn't be right. It's been with me all the way. I can't abandon it now.

I reach towards it but it's too far away. I'm going to have to crawl out there. I know you're not supposed to climb on the unsupported parts of the roof, but I think it will be okay. I'm not that heavy. And it's not as if I have any clothes on to weigh me down.

I climb carefully onto the batts and start moving slowly to the centre. One more metre and I'm there.

I pick up my duck and bring it up to my face. 'Just you and me,' I say.

The duck creaks. That's weird. I didn't know rubber ducks could talk.

Uh-oh. The creaking is not coming from the duck. It's coming from underneath me. The ceiling is giving way.

I try to grab the roof beam but I can't reach it.

The ceiling caves in.

Next thing I know I'm lying, legs spread, in the middle of the dinner table—my fall broken by an insulation batt.

As the dust from the ceiling plaster settles, I see Mr and Mrs Bainbridge and Mum and Dad staring down at me.

Jen is standing next to Dad, her bath towel draped over her shoulder. Her back is turned towards me and she's so busy complaining to Dad that she doesn't seem to notice what has happened.

'. . . I've asked him a million times but he just won't get out . . .' she's saying.

'Oh, dear,' says Mum.

'Oh, my,' says Mrs Bainbridge.

For once in his life Mr Bainbridge is speechless.

It's page 18.

78

'Oh, no,' says Dad, shaking his head at me. 'No, no, no!'

'Oh yes,' says Jen. 'And I'll tell you what else . . .'

I can't find any mechanical bird jokes.

Dad nods in my direction.

Jen stops, turns around and stares.

I cover myself with the rubber duck, swing my legs over the edge of the table and stand up.

'I beg your pardon,' I say. 'I was looking for the kitchen.'

Nobody says anything. They are all just staring at me, their faces and clothes white from the plaster dust.

I head towards the door as fast as I can.

As I'm about to exit I turn towards Jen. She is still standing there, eyes wide.

'Well, what are you waiting for?' I say. 'Shower's free!'

Would you rather? Would you rather?
Would you rather? Would you rather?
Would you rather? Would you rather?
Would you rather? Would you rather?

f you had the choice, Dad,' I say, 'would you rather be eaten by ants or lions?'

'It depends,' he says. He's holding the sauce bottle up to his eye and peering into the neck of it like it's a telescope.

'Blast!' he says. 'It's blocked again!'

'Language!' says Mum.

'"Blast" is not a swear word,' says Dad.

'It's not a nice word,' says Mum.

'Well?' I say. 'Ants or lions?'

I'd rather be fricasseed in bagel crumbs and served in a white wine sauce to wealthy industrialists.

Dad puts the bottle down. He rubs his chin with his hand and frowns. 'I can't say I'm too keen on being eaten by either,' he says. 'Can I have an injection to put me to sleep beforehand?'

'No. You have to be conscious.'

'Hmmm. In that case, I'll take the lions. If I have to experience pain I'd rather it be short and sharp. Ants would take too long.'

'What if the lions were really old, though,' I say. 'And their teeth were all falling out and they just gummed you to death and it took ages and ages and ages?'

WOULD YOU RATHER BE SPLIT IN TWO VERTICALLY?

OR HORIZONTALLY?

'Do we have to talk about this while we're eating?' says Jen.

'It's important,' I say. 'You might be in the situation where you have to choose one day. You'll be a lot better off if you've already thought about it.'

'Yeah, right,' says Jen, rolling her eyes.

Dad is holding the sauce bottle at a forty-five degree angle and poking into its neck with his knife.

'You'll cut yourself if you're not careful,' says Mum.

I'd rather be beaten to death in a bamboo grove by starving poachers and sold off as ointment.

'I'll be careful,' says Dad.

'Dad?' I say, trying to get him back on the topic. I wish Jen and Mum wouldn't interrupt. Dad gets distracted so easily.

'Owww!' Dad slams the bottle down and drops the knife. He's shaking his left hand and grimacing.

'What happened?' says Mum.

what?

'The knife slipped,' he says.

'I told you to be careful. Use the barbecue sauce instead.'

'I don't want barbecue sauce,' says Dad. 'There's plenty of tomato sauce—I just can't get it out!'

'Forget the sauce,' I say. 'Ants or lions?'

'I told you,' he says. 'I'll take the lions but I want good ones. Really hungry, really mean and really quick. One swipe and lights out. No gumming!'

'You can't make demands. You have to take what you get.'

'Then I don't want to sign up.'

'You're already signed up!' I say. 'It's ants or lions. If you don't want lions then you must want ants.'

'No,' says Dad. 'Ants are out of the question.' He turns the sauce bottle upside down and stands it on his plate.

'That will tip over,' says Mum.

'I'm watching it,' says Dad.

'That's what I'm worried about,' says Mum.

'What's wrong with ants?' I say.

'Too slow.'

'What if your body was covered in honey to attract as many ants as possible?'

'Well, honey would attract sugar ants and I wouldn't mind that so much,' says Dad. 'They'd just eat the honey and leave me alone.'

'They'd be all over you, though.'

'But they'd be after the honey—not me.'

'No honey then. You'll be covered in dog food instead,' I say.

'Charming!' says Jen. 'Could you pass the salt, Andy?'

'Say please.'

'Please.'

'Pretty please.'

'Pretty please,' she sighs.

Jen says it because she knows it's quicker to say it than to argue with me about saying it.

'Pretty please with sugar on top,' I say.

'Andy! Just pass the bloody salt!'

'Jen!' says Mum. 'Language!'

'Well, he wouldn't pass the bloody salt.'

'There's still no need to speak like that.'

Jen looks at me through slitted eyes.

I slide the salt grinder across the table.

'There you are, Jen,' I say.

'Thank you.'

'Don't mention it. You're welcome. Any time. If there's anything else you require please don't hesitate to let me know.'

WOULD YOU RATHER... have a pickaxe inserted in the

A: top of your nose?

or

B: fleshy division betwixt your nostrils?

for correct answer see Pg 63.

'There is something else,' she says.

'Anything,' I say.

'Shut up.'

'Jen!' says Mum.

Jen pokes her tongue out at me.

I ignore her and turn to Dad. 'Well? How about it—would you consider the dog food?'

'But I don't want to be covered in dog food!' says Dad. 'If I have to die I at least want a little dignity.'

'But I thought you wanted to die quickly,' I say.

'I do. I'll stick with the lions.'

'What if by covering yourself in dog food I could guarantee you that the ants would finish you off ten times quicker than even the most efficient lions?'

'Now you're just being silly,' says Dad in a loud voice. He's getting heated up. 'You're making promises that you can't keep. I've seen lions. I've seen their claws.'

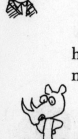

He curls up the fingers on his right hand to demonstrate a lion's claw.

'One swipe can break your neck.'

He swipes his arm across the table so that his 'claw' goes within a centimetre of my nose.

The sauce bottle goes flying. It clatters across the kitchen floor. It comes to rest next to the fridge, spinning slowly.

'I told you that would happen,' says Mum.

But Dad ignores her. 'Are you trying to tell me that ants would be able to kill me faster?'

'You're assuming that the lions will have claws,' I say.

'Well what *do* they have? No teeth, no claws? Are they blind, deaf, dumb and paralysed as well? Why don't I just eat myself and save them the trouble?'

'Now you're the one being silly,' I say. 'Eating yourself is not an option. It's ants or lions.'

Dad shakes his head. He gets up from the table and picks up the sauce bottle.

Jen screws up her face.

'This mashed potato tastes funny,' she says.

'What's wrong with it?' says Mum.

'It's sweet.'

Jen picks up the salt grinder. She examines it closely.

'Does this salt look right to you?' says Jen.

'Pass it over here,' says Mum. She holds the grinder up to the light. 'It's sugar,' she says.

'Andy!' says Jen.

Why do big brothers/sisters automatically blame their little sisters/brothers for everything?

A. Because the brats did it.

B. It makes them feel better.

C. They love watching little kids being punished.

D. A, B and C.

'Yes, Jen?' I say innocently.

'Did you do that?'

'Do what?'

'You know very well what.'

'What?'

'Fill the salt grinder with sugar!'

'No,' I say. It's not a lie, either. I only half-filled it.

Mum sighs. 'Go and get another serve,' she says. 'There's plenty more in the pot.'

'It's not the point,' says Jen. 'He should be punished. Dad, Andy filled the salt grinder with sugar and now my dinner's wrecked.'

'And there's no chance to escape?' says Dad.

'Huh?' says Jen.

'I'm talking to Andy,' he says.

'No,' I say. 'There's no escape. None at all.'

I poke my tongue out at Jen. Dad is more interested in my hypothetical than in her whingeing.

ANTS CAN BE VERY SNEAKY.

'Well, that's not very sporting,' says Dad. 'People don't want to go along and see helpless people being eaten by ants and lions week in, week out.'

'I would,' says Jen. 'Especially if it was Andy being eaten.'

'Nonsense!' says Dad. 'You'd get bored.

You don't scare me

You wouldn't want to go to the footy to see Carlton thrash Collingwood every week, even if you were a Carlton supporter. You need to give the underdog a bit of a chance to keep it interesting.'

'Maybe,' I say, 'but you're assuming it's a public spectacle.'

'It's not?' says Dad.

'No. Nobody's watching. It's just you and the lions. Or the ants.'

Dad looks puzzled.

'Then what's the point?'

'I don't know,' I say, 'but it doesn't matter. The point is to answer the question.'

'I've answered your question,' he says. 'I said I would rather the lions.'

'Is that your final answer?' I say.

'Yes, as long as they're efficient, I'll take the lions.'

'That's not an answer—there's no guarantee.'

Dad picks up the sauce bottle again, turns it upside down and starts slapping the bottom with the palm of his hand. A couple of red drops splatter onto the plate and the tablecloth.

'You'll end up with sauce all over yourself if you don't watch out,' says Mum.

WOULD YOU RATHER?

Would you rather be a

+ PIMPLE
or a
+ BOIL?

WRITE YOUR ANSWER IN 50 WORDS OR LESS AND SEND TO THE MANAGER, STATUE OF LIBERTY, New York, USA.

DO NOT READ THIS NOTICE

This meal is still frozen in the middle.

I am the QUEEN of ORSTRALIA!

I insist that you allow me to be eaten alive by a brace of babbling barred bandicoots.

MOTHER, that sounds fabulous. Count me in, too.

'Jen?' I say.

Jen shoots me a mean look. 'If you're going to ask me whether I'd rather be eaten by ants or lions then forget it.'

'I'm not going to ask you whether you'd rather be eaten by ants or lions.'

'Promise?'

'Cross my heart, hope to die, hope to stick a pin in my eye.'

'Okay, what?'

'Would you rather be eaten by lions or ants?'

Jen points her fork at me. 'You just broke your promise.'

'No I didn't.'

'Yes you did. Now you have to stick a pin in your eye.'

'No I don't.'

Jen gets up from the table.

'Where are you going?' says Dad.

'To get a pin,' she says. Jen turns to me. 'Would you rather a long sharp one or a short blunt one?'

'Nobody will be sticking pins in anybody's eye at this dinner table!' says Mum.

'But he broke his promise,' says Jen.

'No, I didn't,' I say. 'I promised I wouldn't

Go away

88

ask you if you'd rather be eaten by ants or lions.'

'But you did,' says Jen.

'I didn't. I asked you whether you would rather be eaten by *lions or ants*.'

'Same thing!' says Jen.

'No it isn't.'

'Is so.'

'Jen,' I say. 'Whether or not I broke my promise, and whether or not I would prefer a long sharp pin to a short blunt pin or a short blunt pin to a long sharp pin is irrelevant. The real question is whether you would rather be eaten by lions or ants.'

'You broke your promise,' she says. 'And you made me pour sugar all over my dinner.'

There's no point asking Jen. She's too bitter. And Dad is too interested in the sauce bottle to give me a serious answer. That leaves only one person.

'What about you, Mum?' I say. 'What would you rather?'

'Oh, I don't know.'

'What don't you know?' I say. 'It's a very simple question. What more do you need to know?'

'Well,' she says. 'Why is this happening to me? What have I done?'

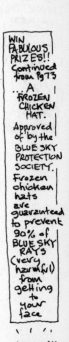

WIN FABULOUS PRIZES!! Continued from Pg 73 ...A FROZEN CHICKEN HAT. Approved of by the BLUE SKY PROTECTION SOCIETY. Frozen chicken hats are guaranteed to prevent 90% of BLUE SKY RAYS (very harmful) from getting to your face

'It doesn't matter!'

'I think it does. If I'm going to be eaten by ants or lions, I want to know why.'

'It's the choice that's important,' I say.

I love eating people. The only meal you can chat to while you eat.

'But how can I make a sensible choice if I don't know why I've been put there in the first place?' says Mum. 'Am I being punished or have I just been picked at random?'

I sigh. Mum can be very stubborn.

'Okay,' I say. 'You're being punished.'

'What for?'

'Mum!'

'Well, I need to know what I've done. That way I can decide whether the ants or the lions are the more appropriate punishment.'

'But how does it change things?'

'Well, suppose I committed a whole lot of small crimes. I think the ants would be the best punishment. But if I did something really bad, something really big—then I think the lions would be the best.'

'Okay,' I say, 'but suppose you did lots of small crimes and a couple of really big ones as well. What then?'

'Then I think both ants and lions would be appropriate.'

'No, but you have to choose one.'

I'm the PAGE NUMBER fly

'But I would deserve both.'

'But which one would you prefer?'

'Prefer?' says Mum. 'I don't like the idea of either option very much.'

Here we go again.

'Cubs would be alright,' she says thoughtfully.

'Huh?'

'Lion cubs. They would be nice. They're very playful.'

'But they're still going to eat you.'

'But they'd do it in a playful way.'

That does it.

'I'm just asking a simple question!' I say, slamming my fist down on the table. 'Would you rather be eaten by ants or by lions? Why can't anybody just answer the question?'

Everybody is quiet.

Everybody except for Dad. He's busy whacking the sauce bottle like his life depends on getting tomato sauce right this minute.

Suddenly sauce explodes from the bottle. It splurts onto his plate, the tablecloth and his clothes. Down his shirt, onto his pants and all over the floor.

He looks at Mum.

'Don't say anything!' he says.

'I wasn't going to,' she says.

I can't help laughing.

'What's so funny?' says Dad, wiping sauce out of his eye. 'Did you have something to do with this?'

Of course I did. But I'm not about to admit it.

'It's not fair,' I say. 'Why do I get blamed for every little thing that goes wrong around here?'

'Because every little thing that goes wrong around here is your fault,' says Jen. 'Punish him, Dad. He gets away with everything.'

'Andy,' says Dad. 'I'm going to ask you a question and I want you to think very carefully about the answer. Tell me, would you rather lose your pocket money for one week or do double chores for two weeks?'

'But you're assuming I'm guilty,' I say.

'I'm not assuming you're guilty—I know it! Now, which would you rather?'

Uh-oh. This is not right. I'm supposed to be the one asking the questions.

'Dad, before I answer, tell me one thing.'

'What's that?' he says.

'If you had to be squashed, would you rather be squashed by bricks or feathers?'

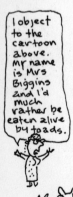

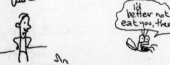

He frowns.

'Don't answer, Dad,' says Jen. 'He's just trying to get you off the track.'

Dad ignores Jen.

'Probably feathers, I think,' says Dad. 'They're softer.'

'But there will still be enough to squash you,' I say. 'Why not choose the bricks? They're not as soft, but they might be quicker.'

'Hmmm,' he says. 'That depends. Would they be dropped all together or one at a time?'

Jen pushes her chair back loudly and stomps off from the table. I don't blame her. We could be here for quite a while.

Murder, bloody murder!

'**M**URDER, BLOODY MURDER!'
I'm yelling at the top of my voice. So is Danny. I look at him. He looks at me. We nod. I take a deep breath.

'MURDER, BLOODY MURDER!' we shout.

Sooty joins in, barking and howling.

We wait. But nothing happens. Nobody comes. No police sirens. My neighbours don't even bother sticking their heads over the fence to check out what the trouble is.

'It's no use,' says Danny. 'Nobody cares.'

I kick a divot out of the lawn.

'It would be too bad if we were really getting murdered,' I say. 'I bet they'd be sorry then. Let's try one more time.'

'Alright,' says Danny. 'Once more and then that's it. I've got a sore throat.'

'MURDER!' we scream. 'BLOODY MURDER!'

'Would you idiots shut up!' says Mr Broadbent. 'I'm trying to work.'

Mr Broadbent is standing in our driveway. Mr Broadbent lives next door. He's a university lecturer. He works in a little room right next to our fence.

'How did you know that we weren't really being murdered?' I ask him.

'Because you've been calling out for the last half an hour,' he says. 'But, I swear, if you don't shut up I'll come back and murder you myself. And your dog!'

Mr Broadbent turns around and stomps back down the drive.

Sooty slinks off into his kennel. Danny and I look at each other. We don't say anything.

We're too scared.

Mr Broadbent has just threatened to murder us.

'Did you hear that?' says Danny.

'I think I did,' I say.

'What are we going to do?'

'I don't know.'

'Should we call the police?'

'I don't think that would be a good idea, Dan. They'll probably arrest *us* for pretending that we were going to be murdered in the first place.'

'But we *are* going to be murdered!' says Danny.

'We weren't *then*,' I say. 'And if we shut up, then there is every chance that we won't be now.'

'But how do we know for sure?' says Danny. 'He's crazy. Did you see the look in his eyes?'

'He did seem a little highly strung,' I say.

'Highly strung!' says Danny. 'That's putting it mildly. He was ready to flip out completely. I know. I've had a lot of experience with these guys.'

'Oh really?' I say. 'When?'

'Just then!' says Danny.

'That's hardly a lot of experience.'

'I watch TV. I can recognise a psycho when I see one. He's going to kill us . . . unless . . .'

'Unless what?' I say.

'Unless we strike first,' says Danny.

'What are you suggesting?'

Danny just stares back at me. 'Do I have to spell it out?'

PAGE 106.

SAY NO TO LAND MINES.

I cup my hands around each side of my mouth. 'Earth to Danny! Do you read me—over?'

'You think I'm crazy?'

'I know it.'

'Well, what do *you* suggest?' he says.

'I think if he's as stressed as he seems then it would be a good idea to help him *de*stress. Cut the problem off at the source.'

'What have you got in mind?' says Danny. 'Elephant tranquilliser darts?'

'I've got the next best thing,' I say. 'Meditation music.'

'Meditation?' says Danny. 'I've never heard of them.'

'They're not a band, you idiot,' I say. 'It's just soft relaxing music. Jen's got heaps.'

I bound up the steps of the porch, go into the house and head towards Jen's room.

Jen is going through this huge New Age thing at the moment. Ever since she went to this New Age & Psycho expo, it's been meditation, chanting, incense and soft music.

I'm sure she won't mind if I just borrow one of her tapes. And even if she does mind she can just meditate and then she won't be angry any more.

PAGE 117.

I open the door of her room.

I'm almost knocked backwards by the stench.

There is a stick of incense burning in a holder on her dressing table. It smells like cat pee.

But it gives me an idea. I grab a handful of incense sticks from the bowl beside the holder. They might come in handy.

I pinch my nose and walk over to her tape collection.

She has every type you can imagine: waterfall, bird-calls, rainforest, wind, breaking waves—you name it, she's got it. The only thing she hasn't got is breaking wind. I guess that's because breaking wind is not relaxing. It's too funny.

I choose a rainforest tape and head for the door before the smell of the incense makes me throw up all over her Yin and Yang rug.

On my way back outside I go to my room and get my ghetto blaster. It's getting old, but it does the job. I just hope the batteries are up to it.

Danny is pacing up and down the back-yard lawn.

'Where have you been?' he says. 'You've

WIN
A FREE
GARDEN
GNOME
(second-hand
with paint
peeling)
QUESTION
continued...
on
different
continents
one fueled
by diesel,
the other
not. Which
one will
get to
YEMEN
first?
Write your
answer on
your budgie
and post it
to: GPO BOX
10011001100
1100110011...

Page 128.

been gone for ages! What if Mr Broadbent had come back?'

'Relax, Danny, I've got a rainforest tape. By the time we're finished the only thing Mr Broadbent will be coming back to do is to hug us for making him feel so good.'

'Yuck!' says Danny. 'I don't think we should make him feel *that* good.'

I set my tape player up on the porch. I insert Jen's tape and press play.

The music comes on. A long, low synthesiser note. It sounds like bird noises over the top, although it's hard to tell. It could be just the squeaking of the tape player's motor.

'Louder!' says Danny. 'It's too soft.'

'It's meant to be soft.'

'Yeah, but Mr Broadbent will never hear it. Turn it up.'

Danny's right. I turn the volume up. It makes it louder alright, but kind of distorted as well.

'It doesn't sound very rainforesty,' says Danny.

'I know, but it's better than nothing.'

'Hey,' says Danny, 'what if we sprayed the hose onto Mr Broadbent's roof? That might help.'

But the story was dropped because it wasn't annoying enough.

BACKYARD OLYMPICS. EVENT 37

Fencing

HOWL!

Page 139. That's it book's over.

Why not? Rain on the roof is a very relaxing sound. How is Mr Broadbent going to know it's not real?

I cross the yard to the tap. The hose is not actually going to reach over to the fence because it's in a huge tangled knot from the last time I used it. And this is no ordinary knot. This is a knot that will take forever to untangle. And we haven't got forever. Mr Broadbent could come rampaging up the driveway any second.

I turn the tap on full blast and drag the hose as far as I can before the knot threatens to cut off the supply. The water makes it over the fence but not onto the roof.

'It's not going to work!' I yell.

'Tighten the nozzle!' calls Danny.

WOOF

A boxer. (P.S. This joke should be on pg. 32.)

I screw the nozzle tighter. That's better. Especially if I point the hose up higher. It makes a perfect arc of water right onto the roof above Mr Broadbent's office. A few minutes of rain on the roof combined with the rainforest tape will mellow Mr Broadbent for sure.

It's risky, though. If the water pressure drops, the water will hit Mr Broadbent's office window. He might think we're doing it to annoy him.

BOOM

Book's finished. You can all go home.

100

Danny gives me the thumbs up.

We're almost out of trouble.

But I don't want to take any chances.

Not when our lives are at stake.

I've still got the incense sticks.

I wave to Danny.

He comes over.

'Danny,' I say. 'I need you to light the barbecue.'

'You can eat?' he says. 'At a time like this?'

'No,' I say. 'I'm not hungry. I want to use it to burn some incense. We can waft the smoke across to Mr Broadbent's house. The smell will help to calm him even more.'

'Anything is worth a try,' says Danny. 'What do I do?'

'Here,' I say. I give him the incense. 'Light the fire and then chuck these on top. If we burn them all at once it will be really intense.'

'Where's the barbecue?'

'In the carport. But you'll need to wheel it closer to the fence.'

Danny wheels the barbecue—half a forty-four gallon drum mounted on a frame with wheels—down to the other end of the drive away from the hose spray. He grabs a branch

FAVOURITE INCENSE FLAVOURS.

Pig's trotter.

Cow Manure.

Green Cheese.

Brussels Sprouts.

LIVE
GUM
LEAF

full of dead gum leaves from the garden and puts it in the top of the drum.

'Got a match?' says Danny.

'Your face and a monkey's bum.'

'Don't joke! This is serious.'

'I'm not joking,' I say.

DEAD
GUM
LEAF

Danny shakes his head. He falls for it every time.

'Just tell me where the matches are.'

'They're under the barbecue.'

He pulls the box out and lights a match. He drops it into the middle of the dead leaves. A thin white strand of smoke rises almost immediately.

LIVE
MATCH

'Quick!' I say. 'Put the incense on top!'

Danny throws the incense on.

DEAD
MATCH

The leaves burst into flame, but the blaze is too strong. The smoke is going straight up into the air.

'It's not working, Danny. You need to fan the smoke across the fence.'

'How?' he says.

'I dunno—use your shirt or something.'

Danny pulls his T-shirt over his head. He starts flapping it wildly. The smoke billows around him. He coughs.

'Is it working?' he says. 'I can't see a thing.'

TICK

We've all got homes to go to. Go on. Clear off.

'Not exactly,' I say. 'You'll have to fan harder.'

Danny goes into fanning overdrive.

The smoke starts heading towards Mr Broadbent's office.

'That's it, Danny! Keep going!'

I can just imagine Mr Broadbent. He's probably sitting back with his feet on the desk. Arms behind his head. Eyes closed as he listens to the calming music and the relaxing rain. Taking deep breaths of soothing incense. Forgetting all about his work, his problems and, most importantly, his threat to murder us.

Danny is piling more leaves onto the barbecue.

'Hang on, Danny, I think that will do,' I say.

But Danny doesn't hear me above the crackling of the fire. He keeps piling on more leaves. Showers of sparks fly into the air. The ends of half-burnt branches are falling to the ground. Danny keeps fanning.

'Danny! Stop it!'

His fanning is sending a torrent of sparks towards the fence. There's smoke everywhere.

Uh-oh. Just as I feared.

Not all of the smoke is coming from the barbecue.

Dad is always saying how he's going to pull the old dead passionfruit vine off the back fence. Well, he won't have to bother now.

'Danny! No more fanning! The vine is on fire.'

Danny comes to his senses.

'Huh? What? Help!' he yells. 'FIRE!'

I remember I'm holding the hose.

I point it towards the fire but it's too short to reach. I try to pull it closer but the water almost cuts off completely because of the tangle.

The flames are leaping high into the air. The whole fence will go up unless we do something fast.

'What do I do?' yells Danny.

There is a pile of fresh grass clippings on the other side of the driveway. They're only a couple of days old. They might help to damp the blaze.

'The grass clippings, Danny! Behind you! Throw them on the fire!'

Danny throws great armfuls of grass all over the fence and onto the barbecue.

It puts the fire out alright.

But now we have a new problem.

Smoke.

Thick, white, eye-watering smoke.

JUST ANNOYING
↓
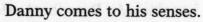

TICK
TICK

My eyes are streaming.

A loud thrumming noise breaks the silence.

I look up and realise that I'm blasting the hose directly against Mr Broadbent's office window.

Big mistake.

And the rainforest tape is starting to sound really weird. It's not only distorted, it's speeding up and slowing down as well.

Sooty is standing at the door of his kennel, barking.

Danny's still yelling. I can't make out what he's saying.

There's smoke and distorted music and yelling and barking and the next thing I see is Mr Broadbent's head—his eyes wide and bloodshot, his teeth bared—and his enormous hands reaching for me through the smoke.

I don't think he wants to hug me, either.

'Do you want to talk?' I offer. 'Talking through your problems can really help . . .'

He doesn't respond.

I point the hose at him and let him have it. No use. It's like firing a water pistol at Godzilla. Mr Broadbent just keeps coming—arms outstretched.

ANGER!! HOW TO IDENTIFY IT.

GLOWING CRANIUM

ROTATING EYEBALLS

NORMALLY BLUNT TEETH BECOME HARD, LONG & POINTY

STEAM FROM NOSTRILS

I'm a PAGE NUMBER FLY.

105

SINGLE HANDED

DOUBLE HANDED

DOUBLE HANDED WITH DOG.

I want to run but I can't move. I'm too scared.

Just as Mr Broadbent's hands are about to close around my neck I see Danny charging up behind him.

He lets out a blood-curdling yell and leaps onto Mr Broadbent's back.

Mr Broadbent roars. He knocks Danny off with one swipe and turns his attention back to me. Danny falls to the ground. He gets straight back up and runs at Mr Broadbent. Mr Broadbent is unfazed. He simultaneously grabs Danny by the throat with his right hand and me by the throat with his left.

I look at Danny. Danny looks at me.

We nod.

We know exactly what to do.

We've practised it many times.

We each take a deep breath and give it everything we've got.

'MURDER!' we yell. 'MURDER, BLOODY MURDER!'

LANGUAGE, BLOODY LANGUAGE!

That's it... I'm out of here.

THE LAST JAFFA

I'm spewing.

James Bond is just about to be eaten by a shark and I'm going to miss it because I can't see past the hair of the woman in front of me.

BIG HAIR PERSON.

It doesn't matter where I sit in a movie theatre, a person with a really big pile of hair on their head will always sit right in front of me. And if they don't, then the tallest person in the world will.

It's not fair. Nobody else has got a big-hair person in front of them. Why me?

'Hey, Danny,' I say, 'wanna swap seats?'

DON'T BE FOOLED

Danny is stuffing his mouth full of popcorn.

'Are you kidding?' he says, spitting little bits of popcorn all over me.

I'm glad I don't have popcorn. Popcorn is for kids. I've got a box of Jaffas. Well, to be more accurate, a box of *Jaffa* because there's only one left.

'Forget it,' I say. 'Dad? Want to change seats?'

'Shush,' he says. 'James Bond is about to be eaten by a shark.'

'I know,' I say. 'I'd really like to see it.'

I know he's not really going to be eaten because he's James Bond and James Bond always escapes, but it's fun to watch how he does it. Well, it would be fun if I could see the screen.

I'd go and sit somewhere else, but the theatre is packed.

'Who's that, Mummy?' says a little boy with a loud voice a couple of rows in front of us.

'A bad man.'

'What's he doing, Mummy?'

'He's going to feed James Bond to the sharks.'

'Why?'

'Because he's a bad man.'

'Why?'

'Shhh,' she says. 'Just watch.'

What kind of person would bring a little kid to a James Bond movie? I have enough trouble understanding all the double-crossings and plot twists myself, and I'm quite intelligent. Well, compared to Danny that is.

I can hardly see anything through all the hair. I lean over towards Danny.

This is one nasty bad man. He's got this trapdoor that falls open onto a pool with a shark in it. If there's somebody he doesn't like he just chains them up, hoists them above the pool and dunks them in. James Bond's toes are only centimetres from the water.

The lady with the big hair tilts her head to the side.

I lean a little further over towards Danny.

She tilts again.

I lean further.

Danny elbows me in the ribs. He does it so hard that my Jaffa is knocked out of my fingers and falls to the floor.

'Keep on your side of the seat,' he says.

'You idiot!' I hiss. 'You made me drop my Jaffa.'

'Have some popcorn,' says Danny.

He shoves the box under my nose. I brush it away.

The Adventures of Jenni Jaffa

THE END.

You shouldn't be here. The book's finished.

109

1

IDENTIFYING
YOUR LOST
JAFFA

①
GRASP IT
FIRMLY
BETWEEN
THUMB AND
FOREFINGER.

②
Turn the
handle
marked
"HOT".

③
Engage the
4WD LEVER
and separate
the two
layers.

④
Kiss the
dog firmly
on the lips

⑤
PUT ON YOUR
HAT + COAT
AND LEAVE
THE SCENE
of the crime
AS INNOCENTLY
AS POSSIBLE
... NOW!!

'No, you don't understand,' I say. 'That was my *last* Jaffa!'

The lady with the big hair turns around.

'Shhh!' she says. 'I'm trying to watch the movie.'

'Tell me about it,' I say under my breath.

'I beg your pardon?' she says.

'Nothing,' I mumble.

I bend over and pat the carpet all around me. No luck. It must have rolled into one of the rows in front.

This is terrible. Trapped behind a woman with big hair *and* I've lost my last Jaffa. And, to make things even worse, I missed seeing how James Bond got out of having his toes chomped by the sharks.

I slump down in my seat.

Life can be very cruel.

It's not like I can just go looking for the Jaffa.

The cinema is packed. I'm in the middle of the centre row. I would have to disturb nine people to get to the aisle. Besides, I can't just crawl down the centre. It would attract too much attention. People might guess what I'm looking for. It might start a Jaffa-rush.

Safer just to sit here and sulk.

Can you please leave the book.

But then I think of how James Bond would react in this situation. He wouldn't just sit here. How did he put it? *A field operative must use every means at his disposal to achieve his objective.* He would go after the Jaffa and do whatever necessary to retrieve it—no matter how great the odds against him—no matter how dangerous.

I'm going to find that Jaffa.

Before I know it, I'm on my belly crawling commando-style underneath a row of movie theatre seats. The darkness makes it hard to see and the danger of accidentally touching somebody's leg is high. But I have to do it.

I have a mission.

It's slow going. My body keeps sticking to the carpet—there must be millions of cups of spilled Coke and Fanta down here. Not to mention all the other stuff. Old chip buckets, ice-cream wrappers, drink cups, lolly boxes, ripped up movie tickets, used tissues . . . everything except my Jaffa.

At the end of the aisle I do a sort of tumble-turn and slip into the next row. There is a forest of legs and shoes for as far as I can see.

Hang on.

I can smell Jaffa.

I wriggle my way towards the smell and stop. It's directly above me.

I can see two small legs dangling over the edge of the seat.

It's the little kid with the big mouth. If anybody knows anything about my Jaffa then he will. Kids and Jaffas go together like ... well ... kids and Jaffas.

I can hear cellophane crackling.

The sound of an engine fills the theatre.

'Why is that man hanging from the aeroplane?' says the boy.

'He's trying to catch the bad man,' says his mother in a low voice.

'Why don't they stop and let him in?'

'Shhh!' says his mother. 'Just watch.'

'That's very dangerous, isn't it, Mummy?' says the boy.

'Shush!'

I roll onto my back. I push myself slowly out to a position where I can see the boy. Just as I suspected. He's got Jaffas. I have an excellent sense of smell.

He's holding them in his left hand. They are resting on the seat beside his knee. The box is almost full. I can see a Jaffa poking out of the top.

I could just reach up and take it. Just
one. It's not my lost one, but it would do.
The kid won't mind. He won't even know.
He's staring at the screen. It's a low thing to
steal lollies off children. Very low. James
Bond would never do that. I would never do
that.

I'm just going to borrow it.

I raise my hand towards the Jaffa. My
thumb and forefinger are poised, like a cobra
about to strike. The Jaffa is almost mine.

'Mummy,' says the kid in a loud voice,
'why is there a boy under my seat?'

I pull my hand back and wriggle back
under cover. Bigmouth strikes again!

'Shhh!' says his mother. 'Don't be so silly.'

'But, Mum,' he says, 'there's a boy under
my seat.'

'I've told you before,' she says, 'stop telling
stories.'

My cover's been blown! I have to get out
of the danger zone. Fast.

I take off down the aisle, elbows pumping.
I bump my head. I burn my knees. I knock
my shoulders. But I keep going until I can't
go any further. I'm caught on a strap. It's
pulled tight under my arm. At the end of the

strap I can see a handbag. And that's not all. The strap is looped around a woman's ankle.

'Hey!' says a voice. A hand with long fingernails reaches down and starts tugging on the strap. 'Help! Someone's trying to steal my handbag. Usher!'

But the harder she pulls the strap, the harder it is to unhook it from my shoulder.

I flop onto my back and push myself out from under the seat to help slip the strap off my arm.

It works. My arm is free.

But now I have an even bigger problem.

Someone is screaming.

'Pervert!'

It takes me a moment to realise that I'm looking up the dress of the woman in the next seat.

Not that I am looking. I'm not. I'm just trying to get rid of the handbag strap. But it's going to be hard to explain the difference. James Bond would know how to do it, but when it comes to the crunch I'm no James Bond. It's safer and easier just to scram.

I pull my head back under the seat and start the long journey back to where I started.

HEALTH WARNING.

MANY OLD LOLLIES ARE DANGEROUS PARASITES.

OLD LOLLIES TO AVOID.

1.
JAFFAS.
Especially those with pre-sucked look

2. OLD FANTAILS.
Especially those with pre WWII actors.

3. MOTH BALLS
THEY OFTEN PRETEND to be Kool Mints.

4. COUGH LOLLIES
Pretending to be JUBES.

on pg 114 You idiot!

Operation find-the-lost-Jaffa has been aborted. I'll be happy just to find my seat.

Too late.

I can see a white torch beam sweeping across the carpet.

The usher!

I can't go forward and I can't go back.

He stops at the end of my aisle.

WIN FABULOUS PRIZES!! (continued from Pg 73)

He is wearing black leather shoes. The shoelaces are tied in big floppy bows. The toes are scuffed. Probably from kicking trouble-makers like me out of the cinema.

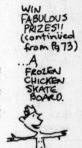

...A FROZEN CHICKEN SKATE BOARD.

'What's the problem?' calls the usher.

'Thief!' gasps the handbag woman.

'Pervert!' says the woman sitting next to her.

How lucky can you be?

'Who me?' says the usher.

'No, under the seat!' says the handbag woman.

'Which one?' says the usher.

I'm breathing hard. Heart thudding.

Any minute now he's going to shine the torch under the seat.

Unless . . .

Brainwave!

Now don't get me wrong. Tying somebody's shoelaces together is on a par with stealing lollies from children. It's not an activity that I

FOOLPROOF
KNOT FOR
TYING AN
ENEMY'S
SHOELACES
TOGETHER.
① Take your partner
by the hand
② Be firm
but gentle
③
④ Relax and reload.

would normally have any part of or recommend to others. But this is an emergency. After all, a field operative must use every means at his disposal to achieve his objective.

I reach out and pluck the end of the usher's shoelace from its loose knot. It unties easily. The lace of his other shoe comes undone just as easily. I tie the two laces together in a simple slip knot. I brace myself. This is it. I spread my fingers apart like I'm steadying myself for the start of a one-hundred-metre sprint.

That's weird.

I can feel something underneath my right hand.

It's small and hard. And round.

Hang on!

I don't believe it.

My Jaffa! I've found it.

Against incredible odds.

I put it in my pocket.

James Bond would be proud of me. I steady myself and prepare to bolt.

'Which row?' says the usher.

'This row!' scream the women in unison.

The usher bends down and shines his torch right in my face.

11

'Good evening!' I say in my suavest James Bond voice and then launch myself right at him and into the aisle.

In his surprise the usher steps backwards. And falls. Ouch!

The torch goes flying.

I'm out in the centre aisle. But in all the excitement I can't remember where I was sitting.

I could yell 'cooee!' and hope that Danny replies, but that wouldn't be too smart. Everyone would know where I am.

There is one way, though.

It's not going to be pleasant but I have to do it. Only my uncanny sense of smell can help me now.

I empty my lungs. I close my eyes. I breathe in through my nose, searching for a particular smell. A particularly bad smell. The worst smell in the whole world. A smell that's kind of a cross between bad breath, dog pooh and garlic.

'He empties his lungs'

Danny's foot odour.

Lucky for me Danny has a habit of taking his shoes off in the cinema. Judging by the smell, it must be about the only time he ever does take them off.

 **11**

Got it! Two rows back to the middle and nine seats across.

Just in time. At least half-a-dozen torch beams start streaming down the aisles.

Backup ushers!

JUST ANNOYING? I don't think so.

I throw myself towards the aisle where the stench is the strongest and dive under the seats before the torch beams hit.

I move smoothly until I get to a seat without any legs in front of it. That must be mine. I emerge and slip back into my place as if nothing has happened.

'Right on!' says Danny.

'Shut up!' I say. 'Just act normal.'

The ushers are patrolling the aisles like prison guards.

I pretend to be absorbed by the movie.

It's not easy. I've completely lost track of what's going on. And I still can't see the screen properly.

All I can make out is that James Bond and his girlfriend are trapped in this enormous factory. It's filled with smoke and fire. Explosions left, right and centre. They are desperately pressing buttons to get the doors open.

My Jaffa!

I have to eat the Jaffa before I lose it again.

I put the Jaffa in my mouth. This is going to be good. I worked for this. I deserve it.

That's funny. I didn't know they made Jaffas with a mint centre. And so chewy.

That's not right. It's not a Jaffa. It's somebody's old chewing gum.

I clutch at my throat. What if the person who last chewed that gum was really sick and now I've got some horrible disease?

I spit the gum out.

It flies through the air, straight into the hair of the woman in front of me.

She jumps up.

'There's something in my hair!' she screams 'Urgh! Chewing gum.'

She turns to me and points.

'You did this, you nasty little boy!'

I slump down in my seat.

The handbag woman stands up.

'That's the boy who tried to steal my handbag!'

The other woman is beside her.

'He tried to look up my dress!'

'No!' I say to them. 'You're making a terrible mistake. That was just somebody who *looks* like me!'

BEWARE of ANCIENT BITS OF CHEWY.
favourite disguises:

1.
As old JAFFA.

2.
As innocent baby's dummy.

3.
As CASHEW NUT

4.
As Pills.

5.
As usher's right eyebrow.

There's a lot of Page 11's in this book.

11

Ushers everywhere. More and more people are crowding around my seat. Nobody seems to be interested in the movie any more.

Even the little kid is standing on his seat and pointing.

'That's him,' he says. 'See, Mummy! That's the boy who was under my seat.'

His mother stands up.

'Is this true?' she says.

Before I can answer, the first usher is shining his torch in my face.

'It's you!' he says. 'The one who tied my shoelaces together!'

The faces of these people appear twisted and evil in the half-light of the movie house. The usher is a dead-ringer for the villain in the film.

I turn to Danny for support.

'Tell them I'm innocent, Danny! Tell them!' I plead.

But Danny's seat is empty. So is Dad's.

They've abandoned me. I can't say I blame them. This is one ugly mob.

'Hey, look, I'm sorry,' I say. 'I'd love to stay and chat but I have to be going . . .'

'Stay right there,' says the usher. 'You're in big trouble!'

BEWARE OF ANCIENT BITS OF CHEWY.

• They will attach themselves to unsuspecting persons.

• They will seek out the moist passages in the body.

• Slowly but surely they will make their way to the brain.

• Gradually they will take over the host's personality

and appearance

Pg 12. That's more like it.

He pushes me back down into my seat.

'Let's speargun him!' says the handbag lady.

People cheer.

'Feed him to the sharks!' cries the dress lady.

Even more cheering.

'Wait a minute,' says a voice. 'Does anybody have a speargun or a shark?'

People go quiet. They shake their heads.

On the screen James Bond has just set a man on fire with a cigarette lighter.

'Let's set him on fire!' cries someone else. 'I've got a lighter.'

'Not in my theatre you don't,' says the usher. 'I'm the one who has to clean up after this.'

These people are obviously mad. Too much James Bond. I have to get out of here.

'Look up there!' I yell, pointing at the roof. 'Ninjas!'

Everybody looks. They're so James Bonded out that they'll believe anything.

It's the chance I need to heave myself out of my seat. But this time I'm not going under— I'm going over. Over the head of the big-hair woman. I use her shoulders as a springboard to leap across two rows into an empty seat. I

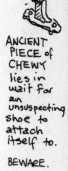

ANCIENT PIECE of CHEWY lies in wait for an unsuspecting shoe to attach itself to.

BEWARE.

12!! WHAT!! 12

Belt of
M+M's
↓

CHURCHOP

TWISTIE

JAFFA

PANTAILS

Aniseed
balls

THE LOLLY
UNIVERSE

use the seat as a trampoline to propel me across another three rows.

An old man tries to hook me around the ankle with the handle of his walking stick. But I grab the walking stick and use it to polevault across the last two rows of seats and up onto the narrow platform in front of the screen.

I look around. Nowhere to go. Both of the front exits are blocked by ushers. And the mob is closing in.

What now? What would James Bond do? He would use every means at his disposal to achieve his objective, of course. If I can't go forwards and I can't go sideways, that only leaves one direction. Backwards. Into the screen!

The hands of the mob are clutching at my feet.

No time to lose.

I jump backwards.

There is an incredible ripping and tearing noise and then everything goes quiet.

It's time
you were
in bed.

Next thing I know I'm lying on a wooden floor.

I can hear cheering and whistling. It's coming from the other side of the screen.

Someone's
tampering
with my
numbers

12

And then I see it. My Jaffa.

And not just my Jaffa. There's hundreds and thousands of Jaffas and old lollies! All the lollies that have ever been hurled at the screen or lost in the history of this cinema have ended up here.

And they're mine.

All mine.

THE
RETURN
OF
THE LAST
JAFFA.

I pick my Jaffa up off the floor. I wipe the dust off it and put it into my mouth. No minty taste this time. Just pure Jaffa.

I reach for another. And another. And another.

My only problem now is how I'm going to eat all these lollies without being sick.

It's going to be tough.

But I can handle it.

A field operative must use every means at his disposal to achieve his objective.

I'll think of something.

SWINGING ON THE CLOTHESLINE

If you've never tried swinging on the clothesline at night then you should. I recommend it.

I've been out here every night for the past three weeks. From midnight to 4 a.m.

But not for fun. I'm in training. I'm going to set a new world record for the fastest ever clothesline swinging. It's my dream.

Unfortunately, my parents don't share my dream. That's why I have to do my training at night while they're asleep. Whenever they catch me swinging on the clothesline they go berko. I've tried to explain to them that I'm not just mucking around, that I'm trying to achieve something special, but it's no use.

'Why can't you play a normal sport like

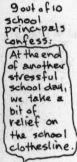

9 out of 10 school principals confess:

At the end of another stressful school day, we take a bit of relief on the school clothesline.

football?' says Dad. 'Something that takes real skill.'

Real skill?

Now don't get me wrong. I've got nothing against football, but anyone can play it. All you need to know is how to run and kick at the same time and you're away.

But breaking the world speed swinging record—now that takes real skill, real dedication and real guts. You need to combine an exhaustive knowledge of aerodynamics with a thorough understanding of the mechanics of rotary clotheslines. You also need to be fit enough to withstand G-forces stronger than most NASA astronauts will ever have to endure. Not to mention being able to run like hell when your parents see you. That's what I call *real* skill.

The bar is cold under my fingers. The wind is cool. There is a slight frost in the air. If I tilt my head back I can see the stars circling above me.

I'm swinging faster and faster. I feel good. I can hear the squeak-squeak-squeak of the clothesline as I spin. I take one hand off the bar and readjust my goggles. Yes, I know that swimming goggles are not the coolest look in

That's better. 125.

125

COPHIN
BROTHERS,
FUNERAL
DIRECTORS,
ADMIT:

we do
it, too

After a
busy day
funeral
directing,
we go home,
into the back-
yard and
fly on the
clothesline.

weeee

the world, but it gets pretty hard to see at the speeds I get up to.

I hear the back door slam.

Uh-oh.

The floodlight comes on and the yard is bathed in bright white light.

Dad is standing there in his dressing gown.

'What do you think you're doing?' he yells.

I would have thought it was fairly obvious, but with parents you can never quite tell. Sometimes they see things very differently to normal people. Best to keep it simple.

'Swinging on the clothesline, Dad. I'm training.'

'Training? I'll give you training!'

Dad grabs hold of the straw broom leaning next to the steps and comes rushing at me with it raised above his head.

I don't think 'training' is exactly what he has in mind. I think 'thrashing' would be closer to the mark.

I haven't got time to get away. This is going to take a bit of fancy footwork. I rock myself back and forth to work up as much extra speed as I can. I wait until Dad is right beside the line. Just as he is about to swing

the broom at me I assume my best Bruce Lee pose and kick the broom out of his hand.

The broom goes flying.

I release my grip on the line, do a spectacular double somersault dismount and hit the ground running.

I sprint up the steps into the house and into the safety of my bedroom.

I push my dressing table in front of the door.

'Open up, Andy!' says Dad. 'I want to talk to you.'

He's rattling the door handle.

'Can't it wait until the morning?' I say. 'I'm trying to sleep.'

'No, it can't,' says Dad. He throws himself against the door like some TV cop trying to break down the door of a TV criminal.

After ten minutes he gives up.

'I'll see you in the morning,' he says, making it sound like the biggest threat in the world. But that suits me fine. By then he'll have cooled down. He might even have come to realise just how serious I am.

I put my head on the pillow and dream of how proud Mum and Dad will be when I set the new world record. They'll come into the

BACKYARD OLYMPICS EVENT 46:

The REVERSE UPSIDE DOWN TOE HANG.

Competitor pegs big toe to clotheshine.

Competitor must hang upside down face out and spin. Last to fall ... wins. NOTE: To save embarrassment you should glue your shirt to your skin.

I'll HOLD MY BREATH.

127 AEC

kitchen and the newspaper will be on the table with the headline: 'BOY BREAKS WORLD CLOTHESLINE SPEED RECORD!' There'll be a big picture of me, swinging on a clothesline in the middle of a huge stadium packed with cheering fans. And I'll just be sitting there eating my breakfast, real cool, and Mum and Dad will be overwhelmed and they'll get down on their knees and beg my forgiveness for not taking my ambition seriously and for placing so many obstacles in my way . . . But I won't hold a grudge. I'll just wave my hand, dab at my mouth with a serviette, stand up and say, 'Hey—no hard feelings . . . we all make mistakes—now if you'll excuse me I have to go and get ready for the street parade that the Prime Minister is putting on in my honour . . .'

WORLD RECORD NUMBER OF PEOPLE ON A CLOTHES- LINE

27 + 1 dog.

The scene that greets me at the breakfast table the next morning is a little different.

Dad is sitting there with an expression on his face like one of those Easter Island statues.

The radio—which is usually burbling away—is not turned on.

KNOCK KNOCK

The sound of my Cornflakes clattering

I'm holding my breath

128.7 FM

into my bowl sounds like a hundred tonnes of boulders falling on top of the kitchen.

'We're very disappointed in you, Andy,' says Dad.

'Yes, Dad.'

'You've let us down.'

'Yes, Dad.'

'I've had to buy three new clotheslines this year and do you know why?'

'Because they're really bad quality?' I suggest.

Dad's ears start wiggling. Wrong answer.

'No!' he yells. 'Because the others were so mangled and broken from your infernal swinging.'

I still think it's a quality issue. If he would buy top of the line, superstrength clotheslines, instead of these crappy jobs made out of nothing stronger than coathanger wire, then we wouldn't have a problem. But I don't say this. Dad is in no mood to see reason. Besides, he's not finished yet.

'Your mother and I have begged you, have pleaded with you, have extracted promises from you—have even bribed you—to stop swinging on the clothesline, but to no avail. I thought we got things straight the last time we talked, but now we discover that you are

C S A
Clothesline
Swingers
Anonymous

Hello, my
name is
Zelda
Sparrow,
I'm 63 years
old and I
am a
Clothesline
Swinger.

Average
Lifespan
of Andy's
Promises?
A ... 15min
B ... 1 day
C ... 4000yrs.
Answer below.

If you
answered ©
you are correct.
Andy is VERY
trustworthy.
If you picked Ⓐ or Ⓑ
you are obviously
a parent.

GASP! 129 × 7 =

$\begin{array}{r} 129 \\ \times 7 \\ \hline 903 \checkmark \end{array}$

sneaking out there in the middle of the night. What have you got to say for yourself?'

'I have a dream . . .' I say.

'You have a what?' interrupts Dad.

POPE CONFESSES!

I too swing on clotheslines

'Nothing,' I say. What's the point of even talking about it? I've explained it a hundred times and they still don't get it.

I push my Cornflakes towards the centre of the table and stand up.

'I'm not really hungry,' I say. 'I've got to get going to school.'

'Not so fast,' says Dad. 'This is the last time I intend to have this conversation. Swinging on the clothesline is to stop and if you think you're going to find that too difficult, then don't worry. I will make it very easy for you.'

'What do you mean?' I say.

'You'll see,' he says with a smile. 'You'll see.'

That's what he thinks.

He'll come soon!

Nothing is going to stop me training. I'm just hitting my peak. What's the worst he can do?

Sit out there all night on guard with a straw broom across his legs? He'll need to sleep sometime.

KNOCK KNOCK

Electrify the line? I'll wear a rubber suit.

OK! You win

Set up a machine gun to spray the line with bullets when it's triggered by a motion sensor? I'll wear Ned Kelly armour.

Nothing will stop me.

I'll see? I don't think so. We'll see who'll see.

That afternoon when I get home from school I walk up the driveway and into the backyard.

Suddenly a huge black dog comes barrelling towards me.

It's massive. Snarling. Long white strings of foam trailing from its bared teeth. And it's heading straight for me.

I clutch the straps of my bag and get ready to bop it across the head. It's not much—like trying to scare off a charging bull with a rolled up tea-towel—but it's all I've got.

The dog lunges for me, but just as it's about to sink its fangs into my neck it is tugged violently backwards. It rears up on its hind legs and flips over onto its back. It has reached the end of its chain, which—as I collect myself—I notice is attached to the clothesline.

I hear laughter from the porch.

'Andy,' says Dad, 'I'd like you to meet Spot. Spot, this is Andy.'

Spot picks himself up from the ground. He lunges at me again.

I jump backwards.

'Are you crazy?' I ask Dad. 'That dog's a killer!'

'Spot? A killer?' says Dad. 'Nah. He's harmless. He just gets a bit touchy when people go too close to the clothesline.'

'You've bought this dog just to stop me swinging on the clothesline?' I say.

'I haven't bought him,' says Dad. 'I just arranged a little swap.'

'You swapped him for Sooty?'

'Not permanently.'

'For how long?'

'For as long as it takes you to break your clothesline habit and develop some new, more healthy interests,' says Dad.

'Like football you mean?'

'Yes, like football—like other boys.'

'I'm not like other boys!' I yell. 'I need something more challenging.'

'Well,' says Dad, 'I think you'll find Spot challenging enough.'

I look at Spot.

132

He's straining on his leash. Staring at me. Just daring me to take one step towards his clothesline.

I've got to admit that at this moment football is starting to look pretty attractive. I'd even consider taking up cricket.

I turn around and go back down the driveway to enter the house by the front door.

I throw my bag hard against my bedroom wall. My pencil case falls out and pencils go flying all over the floor. I pick up a handful and throw them against the window.

Just when the speed record was within my grasp!

From my bedroom window I can see Spot. He is sitting straight-backed, ears twitching, ready to tear apart anyone who is even thinking about going near the clothesline.

Fifty kilos of prime slobbering Dog Power.

If only his power could be harnessed for good instead of evil.

Hang on—that's it!

In the early days of my training I used to get Danny to tie a rope to one corner of the clothesline and tow me around at superspeeds. That was until I was able to generate them for myself and go faster than even

BACKYARD OLYMPICS EVENT 8:

CHOOK CHASE.

1. Let out all of your next door neighbour's chooks.

2. Allow them 5 mins. to settle

3. Now try to get them into his back door. (This is best done while he is out) (The key is under the plaster frog)

The world record for getting 12 chooks into the Kitchen of a next door neighbour is 22 mins.

Good Luck.

Danny could run. But I'm looking at a dog with energy to burn.

If I could slip a harness around Spot and get him to pull me around, I could set a new world record yet. I'll show them!

It's 10 p.m.

Dad is in the kitchen.

'I think I'll go to bed early,' he calls loud enough for me to hear. 'I expect I'll sleep well without the creaking of the clothesline to wake me up—heh heh heh! Anyone for a cup of cocoa before bed?'

'Yes, please,' says Mum.

It's the cue I've been waiting for. The noise of the kettle will block out any noise I make while I'm setting up.

I grab my equipment. Swimming goggles, Sooty's lead and a stuffed toy cat that I borrowed from Jen's room.

I tiptoe down the steps.

Spot is lying with his head on his forelegs.

He might be asleep. It's hard to tell. Are guard dogs allowed to sleep?

I take a step towards him.

He doesn't move.

It's a PAGE NUMBER FLY!

Are they rare?

I take another step.

He remains asleep.

Too easy!

I take another step. I'm now within his range.

He could wake up and chomp me in half, but am I scared?

You bet.

HOW A KNEE SHAKES

HE HE

KNEES SHAKE WHEN THEY HAVE BEEN INFILTRATED BY KNEEMATODES. A KNEEMATODE IS A TINY INSECT THAT HIDES BEHIND THE KNEECAP AND WOBBLES YOUR BONES JUST TO ANNOY YOU.

I place my foot down on the ground as carefully as if I was walking on a one-millimetre thin piece of glass.

My right knee is shaking out of control.

I stoop down to steady it with my hand.

But my hand is shaking as well.

I try to steady my hand with my other hand. But that's shaking even worse. All the stuff drops onto the ground.

Spot opens his eyes.

I can tell by his growl that he is not pleased to see me.

My whole body is shaking.

CATAPULT.

I pick up the fluffy cat and wave it in front of Spot's face. He is mesmerised. I throw the cat to one corner of the clothesline.

Spot is torn.

One eye on the cat. One eye on me.

I'm at his mercy, but I'm counting on the

As hen's teeth.

fact that not even years of specialist guard dog training can overcome a dog's natural urge to chase cats.

I'm right.

Spot lunges at the cat.

There is an explosion of white fluff.

Better that than an explosion of me.

I loop the end of Sooty's lead over the corner of the clothesline above Spot. He's in a frenzy, tearing the remains of the cat apart.

This is my chance.

I sneak up behind him. I grab his neck chain and clip Sooty's lead on to it.

I run to the opposite corner of the line, jump up and hold on.

Spot is still more interested in mangling the cat than in me.

'Hey, Spot,' I call. 'Your father was a sewer rat and your mother was a chihuahua!'

That gets his attention.

He looks up, rears up on his hind legs and starts chasing me.

The line takes off with a whoosh!

Spot is going crazy. They must have starved him for weeks. Either that or he has taken an even greater offence at my insult than I could have predicted.

Whatever the reason, I am swinging faster than I have ever swung in my life.

I'm gripping the bar as tightly as I can. I feel like Superman—arms straight out, head down. I'm going so fast that I'm practically horizontal. The wind is roaring in my ears. I wish I'd thought to put more clothes on. I'm freezing.

The familiar landmarks of the backyard are gone—the shed, the old orange tree stump, the window of the kitchen where Mum and Dad are probably sipping their cocoa right at this moment. It's all just a blur of spinning colour.

Spot is huffing and barking as he chases me around.

Any moment now Mum and Dad are going to hear the racket. They are going to look out of the kitchen window and see me spinning faster than any human being has spun before.

They'll see.

They'll see that I'm serious and that nothing will stop me.

But they're going to have to look soon, because the faster I go the harder it is to hold on. It's like being caught in a force 5 hurricane.

BACKYARD OLYMPICS EVENT 15
HOSE CHOPPING (mechanical)
1. Start up mower.
2. Lay hose on lawn in Pattern A. (see BACKYARD OLYMPIC MANUAL)
3. Pick one path and mow through hose.
4. Count how many pieces the hose is in now.
WORLD RECORD: 342.
Mrs Valda Jones, Rockbank, Vic, Aust. (accidental)

HI MUM.

Z 137

I can't keep this up much longer.
I'm not used to this sort of pressure.
My fingers give out.
I'm flying through the air.
Straight towards the kitchen window.

I'm wondering whether it's safer to crash through a window headfirst or break it with a fist, Superman-style.

It doesn't really matter, I guess.

If the window doesn't kill me, my parents will.